Curtain

Call

Cyberworld Publishing

Cyberworld Publishing

www.cyberworldpublishing.com

This book is copyright © Olivia Stowe 2013
First published by Cyberworld Publishing in 2013
Cover design by S Bush © 2013
Cover photo: © Antonel | Dreamstime.com
E-book ISBN: 978-1-922187-36-9
Print ISBN: 978-1-922187-37-6
All rights reserved

Cyberworld Publishing
Jindalee St
Toronto, Australia

Curtain Call

Charlotte Diamond Mysteries Seven

Olivia Stowe

Table of Contents

Chapter One: Consternation

"Do you suppose that if I told them of my plans, it would relieve their consternation?"

"Don't you dare do that, yet, Brenda Boynton. It will turn them all green eyed with greed."

On their airport layover in Atlanta from Miami, Brenda Boynton, whose stage name as possibly America's premier senior actress was Brenda Brandon, had suggested that her "other," Charlotte Diamond, a retired FBI senior agent, check the messages on her cell phone as Brenda had just spent a half hour doing. Charlotte had avoided the task. She hated the cell phone. As soon as she began to understand how to work one model, another one came out and Brenda insisted that she keep up to date on the technology. Up to date in Charlotte's parlance was when the rotary phone gave over to push buttons, and Charlotte had even resisted that transition until she couldn't carry through on a service call because there was no avoiding the "If this, push that" instruction.

The two were returning to their home in the small Maryland village of Hopewell on the Choptank River from a few whirlwind weeks near the Florida Everglades, where Brenda was filming in a movie and Charlotte had been hired as a movie consultant because there was an FBI angle to the film. As it turned out, there was a much larger FBI angle than anyone had imagined there would be, so Charlotte had worked a bit harder in solving a few sticky mysteries than Brenda had in her supporting role.

But now the two were returning to the "real" world of what had once been a sleepy riverside village populated by a collection of local resident eccentrics and equally eccentric well-heeled and artsy-fartsy retirees. Brenda was connected with the former—albeit marginally—because her family had once been the leading one in the village, and she lived in the family's eighteenth-century manor house on the river that was the town's cornerstone. She had only recently returned there in an unsuccessful attempt to retire from the movies—and, largely, from the world. Charlotte was mostly connected with the retirees by being a retiree herself inserted in the life of the village, although there wasn't an artsy-fartsy bone in her zaftig body.

Charlotte and Brenda having found each other was where these two different worlds of the village intersected. But where Charlotte intersected with everyone in the village was in having been roped in to being the town's mayor. And this was why she was discovering through her phone messages that she and Brenda weren't returning to a quiet village but to one that was in great consternation.

"But if they just could get some assurances that there is something in the offing—" Brenda began to say.

"If they get a whiff at this point how much loot you're hauling home, they'll each have a far better way for you to spend it than on the plans you have," Charlotte interrupted Brenda to say. "We could well have a theme park on the point. No, I think it's best that you get the property bought up first. We'll call Frank and then Scooter when we get home and get some buying under way before others find out about it and try to force up the prices."

Scooter was the somewhat facetious name the parents of Charlotte's Realtor, Scooter Wilson, had given their daughter, and Frank Edmunds was Brenda's financial manager. Brenda, lucky in nearly all things—in addition to being one of the cinema's most beautiful women, even later in life—had won the Maryland lottery to the tune of $98 million while they were in Florida. Luckily she had won it under her real name of Brenda Boynton rather than her movie name of Brenda Brandon, but it was only a matter of time before the world discovered the connection and began to think that she already had quite enough money in her life and should be able to spare some for them.

Brenda had decided on her own that she had enough money and she'd spent much of the recent weeks thinking about what to do with her lottery wins. She was somewhat bemused that she had won; she had just played for the fun and the suspense of it. The plan she had come up with for the money was to build a movie professionals' retirement community on a choice peninsula site at the end of Hopewell's river road. The land had already been bulldozed in another building scheme. The earlier scheme had involved the New Jersey mafia preparing to build an exclusive—and quite illegal—gambling resort on the land, with the guests arriving and departing on yachts via the river.

Before the illegal mob casino plan had been uncovered and scotched, half of the village of Hopewell had already been razed. Scooter Wilson had even been at Charlotte to sell her own riverside cottage in the village to the developers as it was on the edge of the planned resort development. And Charlotte was pondering moving in permanently with Brenda in her colonial mansion farther up River Street.

It was the discussion of living arrangements in Hopewell that had exhausted the two on the flight from Miami even before they were thrown into a longer-than-anticipated layover in Atlanta.

"I wouldn't want to impinge on your independence, Charlotte, but, really, I would be delighted it you were living permanently with me."

"I don't want to intrude on you and assume that you want me around all of the time, Brenda."

It was just this sort of tiptoeing around each other's preferences—when neither had worked this out yet for themselves—and hemming and hawing that drove Charlotte up the side of the plane's fuselage on the Miami-Atlanta flight and that also made her grit her teeth every time they left the village for any length of time together. They still hadn't settled on what "home" was for either of them—or for the two of them together.

Charlotte was grateful that Brenda had finally let the topic drop, even though they had resolved nothing except that where they were both headed today was Brenda's house.

"What is it that the village council members have messaged you about, Charlotte? I could see you grimace and hear you snort, so I guess whatever they are on to you about is giving you great consternation."

"They are the ones suffering consternation. Jason Williams has messaged his dismay. But then he would. As owner of the only garage and filling station in the town, he had been seeing moneybags from the resort plans. Even before you and I left for Florida and as they were tearing cottages down and starting to bulldoze that lot next door to you that you thought you still owned, Jason was already expanding his number of pumps and putting in more repair bays and enlarging his convenience store. I can understand him being very upset, but I got a message from the town clerk, Mary Miller, too. I'm not sure how much new business she and her husband, Walt, expected to get off her beauty salon and his barber shop, but she's got a real mad on about the houses being taken down without a replacement. She's in a dither about property tax revenues and how to make those New Jersey mafia men pay their taxes until the properties can be sold."

"And I could put them out of their misery just by—"

"I can put ourselves out of our misery just by turning my cell phone off. I'm sorry I let you badger me into—"

"I don't badger, Charlotte Diamond." Brenda sat up straight and gave Charlotte the regal stare she had given so often in movies—a pose famous enough that all conversation stopped in the first-class departure lounge and the eyes of everyone were riveted on the movie star, some of the other passengers only now realizing who was in their midst. "I suggest; I don't badger."

The voice was royal indignation, but the sparkle in Brenda's eyes gave her away. She was clearly having Charlotte on.

Charlotte reached over and placed a reassuring hand on Brenda's forearm to show her that they weren't really in an argument, which they rarely were, as the two adored each other and appreciated and celebrated any differences they had. She would have liked to show even more affection, but they were hardly in a venue where she could do that—not for her reputation, of course, but for Brenda's. Any sign of anything beyond mere friendship between them, and cell phone photos would snap off and Hollywood tabloids would roll out of presses.

"Nonetheless, it can all wait," Charlotte countered as they heard their flight from Atlanta to Baltimore-Washington International being called. "We are leaving the wreckage of international espionage, forty-year-old murder cases, and general mayhem on that movie set back in Florida. A little bit of worry over gas station customers and property tax revenue can hold on for a bit longer. Buy up the property first. The city council will be delighted that there's a solution to this, and they can wait a couple of weeks to be delighted."

"All right, then," Brenda said, with a sigh, as she rose from her seat, everyone in the room now following every movement of the screen legend in their company. And not a few of them were sighing as well at the pleasure of being in Brenda's physical presence. "I guess first things first. I'll first be concerned about how we're getting home from the airport. I still think you should have let me park my car at the airport."

"Yes, that would have been good. That would have blown every bit of your $98 million windfall in replacing the Jag; it would have been stolen from that lot before we took off for Miami," Charlotte said, with her signature snort. "Don Dunkel volunteered to pick us up at the airport. He had an ecclesiastical conference to go to in Baltimore anyway. And he can fill us in on the tension in Hopewell over this construction business. At least he will have a level head about it."

The two were about to enter the gate when Charlotte's cell phone went off again. She had thought she had turned it off, but she was still trying to learn the mysteries of this instrument—and the cell phone wasn't helping her. She took a look at the caller's ID, fully intending just to turn the phone off and continue on, but the name that popped up arrested her movement.

"Go on ahead," Charlotte said. "I should take this." Then she said "Just a minute please" to the caller and watched Brenda being royally escorted into the tunnel connected with the airplane.

"Hello, Evan," she said when Brenda had disappeared. "I'm about to get on a plane, so I can't talk."

"I just want to welcome you home," Evan Worthington said in his smooth baritone voice from across the miles. "I thought you'd be back in Maryland by now."

"There was a delay. There's always a delay," Charlotte answered. "We're still in Atlanta."

"Well, welcome to Atlanta then and home later," he said in his confident, melodic voice. "I'll call you again when you get home. I want to see you again."

"Evan," she started to say, but an attendant was there at her side, entreating her, as the last of the first-class passengers, to board so that they could open boarding to economy class. "Never mind. I have to go now . . . but thanks for calling."

She felt like a heel as she trudged down the tunnel to the plane. She felt a little dirty for waiting until Brenda was out of sight before answering Evan's call. Brenda was all she wanted in life. There wasn't a doubt in her mind about that. So, why was she so secretive about Evan? She filed this lunacy away to worry about later.

As the two women entered the baggage claim area at Washington-Baltimore International Airport to pick up their luggage, Charlotte could see the consternation on the face of the village Episcopal priest of their village chapel from across the room. His face lit

13

up in a smile when he saw them, but the expression he'd had before that was impossible to miss.

"Here we are, Don. I hope you haven't been waiting too long," Charlotte said as the paths of the three intersected and Dunkel reached for a couple of pieces of luggage.

"No, I barely made it here now myself," he answered. "Traffic on the Baltimore-Washington Parkway was much worse than I anticipated."

"You looked worried when we first saw you," Brenda said. "Problems at the conference?"

"Not really, no," he answered. "Problems in the village. It's been devastated by the collapsed resort construction. And in anticipation of that the dioceses had approved an expansion of the sanctuary. I've just learned that the construction contract is binding unless we pay a hefty penalty, and they've already started work anyway. Many of the village have overextended in anticipation of the resort. I just don't know how . . . well, I can say that I'm certainly glad our mayor is back."

"Terrific," Charlotte muttered under her breath.

"Beg pardon?" Dunkel said.

Charlotte was about to say something sarcastic when Brenda nudged her in the ribs.

"It's good to be back, Reverend Dunkel, despite the problems we face," Brenda, ever the diplomat, said. "And the village couldn't be in better hands than Charlotte's at a time like this. Let's get back to Hopewell and see where we can get started."

Her smile was dazzling, and Don Dunkel was as mesmerized as all men—and many women—were in Brenda's presence. He beamed back, looking for all purposes as if having completely forgotten his worries for the village.

"Terrific," Charlotte intoned again, but she already was walking away toward the exit, rolling a big suitcase behind her, the ultimate independent woman, having refused all offers of help from friends and attendants alike, so neither of her companions heard her say once again how thrilled she was to be back in Maryland.

* * * *

"Oh, s—sassafras," Brenda said as they motored along in Don Dunkel's vintage big black Buick. Charlotte was snapped out of her reverie of wondering if all Episcopal ministers drove big black Buicks and, turning, looked over the front seat and into the back where Brenda was sitting. Brenda gave her a sloppy grin and nodded toward the back of Dunkel's head.

"What is it, Miss Congeniality?" Charlotte asked, with a sweet smile.

"Bea. I was to let her know when we were coming home. I was to give her warning." Brenda was referring to Bea Helgerson, long-time village resident Hannah Helgerson's niece. Bea was the superefficient housekeeper and cook extraordinaire they had hired shortly before leaving for their movie shoot in Florida.

"She'll just be up on Spring Street with the dogs, staying at her aunt's. We'll call her and ask her to bring Sam and Rocket down to us." Sam and Rocket were their dogs by default. Sam was a Siberian husky, which a good many months previously Charlotte had been watching for her neighbors who were thought to be on an archeological dig but who, instead were in a car at the bottom of the Choptank. And Rocket was the boxer originally belonging to another neighbor, living at the point at the end of River Street, who was a master spy and pulled off his own disappearance, leaving Rocket behind. Both orphans had been taken in by Charlotte and Brenda, who treated them like the children the two never would have and who, in turn, were worshipped by the dogs.

"But she'll not have fixed anything for us to eat for dinner," Brenda said. "That's the point that has me kicking myself."

"Not a big deal," Charlotte said. "I'll whip up something. There's surely something in the frig or pantry I can fix."

There was a moment of silence, and then Don Dunkel cleared his throat and said, "You both certainly are welcome to come to the rectory for dinner tonight. I'm quite sure that Mary won't mind." The Episcopal priest, who was a widower, had the second best housekeeper in the village in Mary Sparks.

Charlotte looked into the backseat at Brenda, who was doing everything she could not to laugh out loud.

"Thank you, but—" Charlotte started to say.

But Brenda couldn't hold back any longer. She interjected a, "Thanks, Don, but it's too late in the day to wish us on Mary for dinner. We'll just pop in to Zenna's for a bite. We're not really that hungry."

Charlotte gave her a "speak for yourself on who is hungry and who isn't look," but she was on the verge of laughing herself. Brenda well knew that Charlotte was ready for something to eat at any moment of the day. But she hadn't thought before she'd said she would fix something for them to eat—and Don Dunkel had revealed that he and most of the village knew Charlotte was a lousy cook. He'd offered to spare Brenda the risk of food poisoning.

16

As they were driving into Hopewell, they passed the last farm before town, which was known as Clagett's farm after the last family that had lived there before it had gone vacant until an eccentric recluse who had been Brenda's sometime housecleaner, Edith Smith, had rented the place. Shortly before Brenda and Charlotte went to Florida for the movie shoot, Edith's criminal lookalike cousin, Ida, murdered Edith—or so the authorities believed—dropped her into the farm's well, assumed her identity, and now was on the lam. The elusive Ida Smith had been the object of one of Charlotte's last FBI cases—and one of the only ones she hadn't closed—before Charlotte had retired as a senior investigator in the FBI's Annapolis office and moved to Hopewell.

A man in his late fifties—much the same age as Brenda and Charlotte—but well-muscled and obviously well-preserved and exercised was at the edge of the farm's driveway, driving a hole for a mailbox post.

"Why that looks almost like Kevin. But—" Brenda began to say.

"Yes, that's Kevin Clagett," Don broke in. "Returned to reclaim the family farm."

"He sure looks good," Brenda said. "But he always was a handsome devil. I remember high school when Joyce Purcell and I fought over him and all of the other girls in town wanted him too." By Joyce, Brenda was referring to the neighbor still living across the street from her, Joyce Vale now, who, along with her husband, Todd, owned and ran the River Street Hopewell House Inn B&B.

"I can see what you mean," Charlotte said with just a bit of jealousy. "He's a real hunk." But it also was a bit of embarrassment, as her mind went to the current head of the Annapolis FBI office, Evan

17

Worthington, who had been Charlotte's lover for a short time when they had both been in training at Quantico, Virginia, decades earlier. Since Even had taken over the Annapolis office, he had been pressing Charlotte to return to work as a consultant and had also tried to wine and dine her. But Charlotte had decided to take a different path in life—she was with Brenda now. That, unfortunately, didn't mean that she didn't still feel conflicted concerning Evan from time to time.

Brenda continued her reminiscences of Kevin Clagett. "I think much of his appeal was that he was such a bad boy. I can remember when he and a couple of other boys took the vice principal's car on a joy ride and even tried to sell it in Cambridge. And none of the boys even had licenses. All of their fathers were important enough in the county, though, that nothing came of that. I often wondered if he got into more trouble later, because he just sort of disappeared after school. I heard he went into the service, but who knows about that? Do you know, Don? You were around then; just had gotten out of seminary, as I recall."

"I wouldn't be surprised if we didn't really want to hear where Kevin Clagett has been all these years," the minister said. And by the way he cleared his throat, both women got the message that he didn't want to follow that discussion any further and that he quite possibly had knowledge that his position prevented him from sharing.

"But does he know about the farm?" Brenda asked.

"About the body in the well?" Charlotte added.

"I presume so," Dunkel said. "A well company truck was out in back of the house all last week. Sinking a new well, I presume. But no one is sure. You know the Clagetts. I think the old well was dry, so they only have to go down deeper than that and the water should be OK."

"Always the quiet ones," Brenda said. "Every single one of them."

"Not anymore," the pastor answered with a twinkle in his eye, as he passed between Brenda's Federal mansion—the oldest and largest building in the village and once the main house for the plantation that had covered this side of the Choptank River for more than a mile—and the Vales' B&B. They were driving on past the house, because Charlotte had asked him to take them to Hannah Helgerson's house so that they could alert Bea they were home and could collect their dogs. Both Charlotte and Brenda were anxious to see Sam and Rocket again.

"What do you mean he isn't quiet anymore?" Brenda asked.

"It's not Keith who's not the quiet Clagett anymore, but I think I will let you discover that for yourself," Dunkel answered. "There's only so much gossiping a man of the cloth should be doing in his own parish."

But both Brenda and Charlotte had stopped paying attention to what the pastor was saying now as they had reached the turn to the left on Main Street. They were both looking beyond that point toward the peninsula at the end of River Street, where the end of Hopewell jutted out into the Choptank River. It looked like a war zone from that point further, with the only building standing being Charlotte's own cottage on the right, on the riverfront. Those hoping to build a resort casino there had nearly leveled the former secluded, heavily wooded house and lot on the point to red clay, leaving only some of the extensive landscaping Win Engleton had put around his house to enhance privacy. The house beyond Charlotte's, which had belonged to her neighbors, the Wellses, who had wound up in the drink, was a pile of rubble, and the three houses that had been on the land side of the street going down

19

to the walled point estate had been reduced to roofs flat on the ground on top of collapsed walls.

"Oh, my," Brenda said. "I had no idea they got this far along in the bulldozing."

"Rather disheartening, isn't it?" Dunkel asked in a somber voice.

"I can see why I'm getting all of those phone calls on the village being ruined," Charlotte said.

"Particularly since, in anticipation of the resort being built here, most of the village's businesses invested in adding facilities and services and inventory," Dunkel said. "Even the church."

"Should we tell him?" Brenda whispered to Charlotte across the car seat. Dunkel, of course, could hear her just as well as Charlotte could, but he was well trained not to pry.

"I think we must wait until we've talked with Frank and have seen what can be done." Charlotte was referring to Frank Edmunds, Brenda's financial administrator. It didn't matter how much discretionary money winning the lottery had brought Brenda. If no one was selling the land, she couldn't put her plans to develop it into action.

Nothing further was said, because they had pulled up in front of Hannah Helgerson's house on Spring Street, extending from the short couple of blocks of businesses on Main Street. They weren't making a quiet entrance; they could clearly hear the excited barking of two dogs from inside the bungalow. Sam and Rocket knew their mistresses were home. The door to the house opened at the same time that Charlotte and Brenda opened their car doors, and the husky and boxer bounded out of the house and were jumping all over the women, very democratically switching from one to the other.

"My lands, it's Miss Brenda and Miss Charlotte," a short, plain, roly-poly woman in a sack dress and apron and a glorious smile said as she came out of the house and down off the porch. "I'm sorry, I didn't get your message you were coming home so soon."

"I'm the one who is sorry, Bea," Brenda said. "I neglected to send it."

"I'm afraid there's little at the house. I'll have to—"

"Don't worry about that," Brenda said, "I'll go pick up enough to last us through lunch tomorrow and you can go shopping tomorrow morning. Go ahead and spend the night with Hannah. We'll be fine. We'll take the dogs with us now, though."

"And a good thing too," Bea answered with a laugh. "They've been angels right up to the time they knew you were here. I don't think there would be any keeping them away from you tonight."

Charlotte was speaking to Dunkel. "Don't worry about the village, Don—or even the expansion plans on your sanctuary. I think Brenda has a plan to fix that—and, if that doesn't work out, we'll come up with something else, I'm sure."

"It's good to have you back, Charlotte. I know you sort of got bamboozled into being mayor, but you are a steadying influence here. I think things will be just fine for a while. And I hope it will be a long while before you are off again. But that's just selfishness talking."

"I think we'll be staying put for the foreseeable future, Don. I think Brenda has been cured of the acting bug for a while, and she has something in mind that will keep her pinned down here for a year or more. Probably more. Thanks for the ride from the airport. Since we're stopping at Zenna's for dinner we'll take the dogs and you can leave us here and we will walk to Zenna's and then back home. We've been

21

cooped up on airplanes all day. The walk will do us good and it isn't far."

"I'll put your luggage on the front porch of your house," Dunkel said.

They both knew the luggage would be safe there in this small village, something that could not be counted on in a larger town. And Charlotte liked the sound of the pastor calling Brenda's house hers as well. For a small town, the people here had been amazingly tolerant of two women living together in something far more intimate than a celibate arrangement of two middle-aged (but, truth be known, slightly older than that) women without men. Neither was remotely celibate when it came to each other. Luckily—and amusingly to both Charlotte and Brenda—many didn't even consider that could be an aspect of their relationship.

Zenna's, the full name of which was Zenna's Russian Bakery, was located on River Street at the corner of Main Street half way back to Brenda's house. The bakery that also served coffee and tea had three tables for "eat-in" customers. In a village like Hopewell, that was all it needed, although the tables often were filled and, in good weather, there were a couple of tables out on the sidewalk too. The bakery occupied one corner of the village's community center, which at one time had been its small elementary school.

Zenna, originally a Russian national—and Charlotte had no idea of her current national status and had no interest in looking into that— was a good baker, hardworking, and as friendly as they came. When Charlotte and Brenda had left for Florida, Zenna had been holding down the bakery alone, and it had been quite a job for one woman. Now it appeared that she had hired someone to help her.

A small, trim dynamo with red hair and of indeterminate age, somewhere between her upper forties and late fifties, met the two women at the door. She had menus in her hand and it was obvious that she was there to serve. Charlotte and Brenda looked warily at her, each holding the leash of one of their dogs and wondering if they would be denied entrance with pets—the dogs would have howled to be left alone out on the sidewalk leashed to a patio table when they had just now been reunited with their mistresses.

But the woman just looked at the dogs and, without batting an eye, said, "A table for two plus two?"

"Yes, please," Brenda said, and they were led to one of the three tables in a whirlwind of service, just like this was a busy city restaurant even though they were the only patrons at this time.

"Will this table suit?" she asked.

"It's perfect," Brenda said, both woman trying to repress chuckles.

The woman had seated them, taken their orders, appeared with their drinks and with something for Sam and Rocket to gnaw on, and had rustled up their sandwich orders and was back scrubbing down the bakery counter within minutes, all with Brenda and Charlotte watching on in amazement at her energy and efficiency.

Zenna put in an appearance from the bakery's kitchen at the back while Brenda and Charlotte (and Sam and Rocket) were eating and discussing what was facing them in the way of settling-back-in domestic chores over the next few days.

Brenda stepped up to the schedule first. "If you'll walk the dogs before you get home, I'll drive out onto Highway 50 and go to the market at the Sheetz gas station. Then I don't know about you, but I'm exhausted and need the bed."

"I'll call my Realtor, Scooter Wilson, tomorrow and see if she's handling the offering on the land on the point," Charlotte said, "And you can call Frank Edmunds and start working your financials. I am, of course, quite willing to sell my cottage to you for the project—if, of course, you don't mind me moving in with you permanently. Or, I, of course, could buy a lot out Spring Street and—"

"Of course I want you to live with me, Charlotte," Brenda said. "I've wanted that for some time. I want you with me, in our bed."

This was the strongest declaration from Brenda that Charlotte had heard thus far, and it almost moved her to tears. She was reaching over to touch Brenda's forearm affectionately when she sensed Zenna entering the room. She hesitated only momentarily before going ahead and completing the movement.

Zenna stopped momentarily to talk to the red-headed woman at the counter. They both looked in the direction of Brenda and Charlotte, and Zenna obviously was informing the other woman where the two fit in in the village. And then Zenna was approaching the table, not batting an eye at the affection Brenda and Charlotte were showing toward each other. The two women had kissed while Zenna was en route.

Zenna pulled over a chair and sat. She was dusted with the flour of tomorrow's offerings.

"I hadn't heard you were home," she said. "I hope things went well in Florida with the movie."

"Other than a murder or two," Charlotte answered. Zenna just laughed, not pursuing the issue further. Murder had seemed to find the retired FBI agent often since she'd moved to town. Zenna had had a pretty adventuresome life herself, the details of which she hadn't shared with anyone in the village, and she found Charlotte serving as a magnet for mystery interesting, not disturbing. "And this is only our second stop coming home—even before Brenda's . . . our house. The first was to pick up Sam and Rocket, of course."

"Then you haven't heard all of the sob stories yet," Zenna said to Charlotte, obviously referring to Charlotte's position as the village mayor.

"I have a cell phone, so, yes, I've gotten lots of calls. None from you, though."

"Only because I didn't know your number," Zenna said. The three laughed, but Brenda and Charlotte could tell there was a bit of strain behind Zenna's laugh.

"Has the collapse of the resort construction affected you too?" Brenda asked.

"I was moving the bakery to Main Street," Zenna said. "A bigger place. Where the Maryland House restaurant was. I'm committed to the lease for several months, I'm afraid and already had put in some improvements. And as you can see, I hired help."

"Yes, she's quite a piston," Charlotte said. "Fast and complete service. And quite friendly. But she's new in town, isn't she? I don't think I've met her before."

"Yes, she's new. That's Evonne Clagett."

"Clagett?" Brenda answered.

"Yes. She's married to Kevin Clagett, who has moved back to the Clagett farm. She's fit right in. Already knows everyone and has already given advice to everyone on improving their lives. I would say something to her about that, but she always seems to be right on and everyone has appreciated the advice. And you're right. She's a great worker. Probably too good for this small bakery. But she needed the job. I'm just sorry that I won't be able to keep her on . . . now."

"Take heart, Zenna," Brenda said, touching the other woman's arm. "There are possibilities yet of developing that land and bringing more business into the town."

"I certainly hope so. It looks terrible now, and this was such a pretty little village. That's what had attracted me to this place."

Both Brenda and Charlotte thought there was much more to the story of how the Russian woman ended up in Hopewell, but neither one had pried into that and didn't plan to now. They had finished their dinner and knew it was time to move on.

They split up out in front of the bakery, with Brenda turning north toward her Federal mansion across the street and Charlotte and the two dogs moving south toward the point. She wanted to check on her own cottage, and the bulldozed land at the end of the street was a perfect place to walk Sam and Rocket. Twilight had fallen, and it was dark on the street. The village was too small to have street lamps except on the two-block main business street, although some of the houses, including Brenda's, had lamps on poles down at the street.

The dogs were prancing merrily along until after Charlotte had checked her cottage and come out onto River Street. Then the two lifted their heads, began to bark, and, together, pulled her toward the middle collapsed house across the street from hers.

Charlotte wondered what had attracted them until she too saw the light of a flashlight, which switched off as soon as it was apparent that Charlotte and the dogs were headed in that direction.

26

Charlotte came around the side of the collapsed house in time to see the gleam of moonlight reflecting off metal and the fleeting image of a figure in dark clothing disappearing into the tree line at the back of the lot. She clicked the flashlight she was carrying on and found fresh shovel marks at the back edge of the wreckage of the house. Moving around the house she saw that this wasn't the only place where recent digging had been going on.

Yet another mystery, she thought. Not back in Hopewell for more than two hours and already there was another mystery facing her. She was either blessed or cursed, she thought. Cursed, because she was trying her best to retire from sleuthing, but possibly blessed because, as Brenda kept telling her, she was energized by a good case to solve—and, she had to admit, a lot easier to live with during those periods. When she had retired, she had assumed that she now had time to read all of the nineteenth-century romance novels that had intrigued her in the abstract. She had found that they weren't all that special in reality, but had denied this for a long time before Brenda had pointed it out. Sometimes Charlotte thought that Brenda knew her better than she knew herself.

As she neared Brenda's house, she saw that Brenda was still there, standing at the entrance of the detached garage. Just standing there and looking in the open door.

"It's gone," Brenda said in a small voice as Charlotte approached.

"What's gone?" Charlotte asked.

"The Jag is gone," Brenda said in a disbelieving voice, referring to her vintage Jaguar XK-E sports convertible. "You didn't want me to

27

leave it parked in the airport lot because it might be stolen there, so we left it at home. And still it's gone."

Charlotte sighed. Yet another mystery. "It's too late to raise the police on it tonight. Who knows how long it's been gone? Take my Escape for now and let's turn in as soon as you get back. We'll start picking up the pieces of reality tomorrow." She watched as Brenda got in the Ford Escape and pulled out of the garage.

So much for property being safe in a small village like this, Charlotte thought. And, somewhat more resentfully, she went on to note that the thieves had been selective—taking the fancy Jaguar and leaving her more pedestrian Escape. She turned to the house with Sam and Rocket straining at their leashes to get into the house—wondering and hoping that the luggage hadn't also been stolen from the front porch where Don Dunkel would have left it.

Chapter Two: A Worrying Possible Presence

"Yep, it's gone all right. A classic Jag roadster shouldn't be too hard to find, though."

"We didn't really need you to tell us Brenda's car was gone, Dave," Charlotte said. She and the hunky young deputy sheriff of the county, Dave Burch, the top of the most wanted list of nearly every single woman in the county—and some of the married ones as well— were standing in front of the open, and empty, bay of the detached double garage behind Brenda's house. Charlotte's Ford Escape was in the other bay. The two weren't jousting. This was just the way they liked to banter. Charlotte's skills and experience were highly prized by Burch. She'd eased the way to the solution of a good many crimes in the short time she'd lived in Hopewell. When the sheriff's office was called for anything happening in Hopewell, it usually was Dave Burch who was going to show up. The sheriff's department had the country sectioned in quadrants, and Hopewell fell into the quadrant Burch was assigned to cover. And everyone in Hopewell was pleased that it was Burch who responded. They felt safe with him—or at least everyone in the village who wasn't hiding something at that moment did.

"By now it could be in Mexico," Charlotte said. "We were gone for a few weeks. It could have been stolen the day we left."

"True. But if it's on the Eastern Coast, we'll find it. Of course, from what I've heard Ms. Boynton can buy a couple hundred more of those if she wants."

"I think the problem is that there aren't too many more of those to be had and Brenda loved that one. So, you've heard about the lottery win?"

"Yes. First thing the lottery folks did was notify us that the winning ticket was from a store down here. There weren't that many tickets sold there, and old Ben at that store kept records on who he sold the tickets to. I was over here pronto to make sure that Ms. Boynton wasn't needing the county's protection yet, but you two were already off filming your movie. Wish I could have gone with you. I've always wanted to be in the movies."

"Believe me, Dave, there are women around here who would like to see you in the movies. But we need you right here holding the county down." She'd had a few glancing blows off the question of the total integrity of the county's sheriff, Haws Wainwright, before, and it was always Dave Burch she wanted to see when there was trouble.

"Is Ms. Boynton coming out to fill in the paperwork?" Burch asked.

"Not unless she has too. She says she's happy to leave crime to me. Can I fill out what I can and then take the rest of it to her to finish and sign? She's in the backyard taking her anger out on deadheading roses. She's waiting for her financial administrator to show up and then she'll be closeted with him much of the rest of the day."

"I don't see why we can't work it that way. So, is she trying to decide what to do with the lottery money?"

"I think she's already decided—and, yes, that's what Frank Edmunds is here for. And, Dave, if you can bear with me, I'd like you to take a walk up toward the point when we're done with the paperwork on the car. I think we have another little mystery on our hands the sheriff's department should know about."

Burch grinned. "Sure thing. It's great having you back home, Ms. Diamond. Police work can be a bit dull around here when you're gone. You always have the most interesting mysteries to share. And here you aren't back a full day yet and you've got at least two mysteries going."

"And maybe a leftover third, Dave. Unless you caught Ida Smith while we were gone. We left you having just accomplished the identification of the body of her identical cousin, Edith, found down the well at Clagett's farm. Has Ida been caught, or has the sheriff's department come up with some other explanation of what happened? We were quite sure that Ida was assuming Edith's identity, although she would have had to take on a whole lot of strange quirks."

"No, we're still sure you were right on that one. And she hasn't been apprehended yet, although we get reports of sightings of her here and about, so she still may be in the area."

"Well, don't feel bad about not catching her yet. I tried catching her my last two years with the FBI office and she always managed to slip through my fingers." Charlotte sighed. "About Clagett's farm. I understand there's a Clagett back on it."

"Yes, Kevin, the last of the Clagetts as far as I can tell. He's come home. It's good to have someone in the place. Abandoned murder scenes seem to breed interest and vandals that the police are kept busy following up on."

"So, where has this Kevin been all these years?"

"Beats me. But I've heard he was quite a cutup when his family lived here. A lot of brushes with the law. It wouldn't surprise me if he was doing some time. But have you met his wife, Evonne, who is working at Zenna's? Now she's a real firecracker. She's already into everything and knows everybody. I think she probably has more energy than Zenna's can handle."

"Yes, we met her last night. Quite vivacious. And she seems to be very capable. I've already started scheming how to make her mayor of this town."

They both laughed at that. Burch knew how Charlotte had been duped into taking the mayoral job that nobody else wanted and that she'd had no idea how onerous it would be.

"But enough gossiping about the neighbors," Charlotte said, turning more serious. "I can't keep you on this all day. So, show me that paperwork we have to do on the missing Jaguar now and then take a walk with me."

"A walk would be good," Burch said. "Covering the county by car as we do, I don't get nearly enough exercise."

Charlottes begged to differ. Dave Burch looked like he got just the right amount of exercise. But she didn't say anything.

"Just give me a moment to let Brenda know where I've gone."

Charlotte rounded the corner of the house and had to smile at the vision of Brenda in an old plaid shirt and loose trousers and a floppy sunhat attacking the dead hips of roses in her garden like she had a grudge against them. She was wearing the heavy Wellington boots that

Charlotte just couldn't get her to replace with something less clunky. And still, in spite of this garb, she looked like the movie star she was.

"I thought I'd hidden those boots," Charlotte said, as she walked up to Brenda.

Brenda turned to her and smiled wanly. She stood up straight and took a swipe at her brow with the back of her hand. Charlotte almost ached at how naturally beautiful the woman was even in her frustration at the disappearance of her beloved Jaguar roadster.

"I found the boots. They go right back into the closet," Brenda said. "This back lawn is marshy, especially after the rain we've had, and these boots are perfect for the purpose in this yard."

"They are so heavy and clunky that I'm surprised you can lift your legs," Charlottes said, with a laugh. "But I came back here to let you know that I want to show Dave something up the street. And I'm taking Sam and Rocket with me."

"Fine. Frank Edmunds should be here to go over the financials of our plan when you get back. In the meantime, I'm going to continue treating these dead rose heads like I'd handle whatever thieves took my car—if I could lay my hands on them."

"You certainly won't be chasing them in those boots. But I'm glad you've found a useful avenue to channel your justifiable anger and frustration."

As Charlotte walked back toward the garage by way of the house to gather up the two dogs, both excited at the prospect of a walk, she thought once again that she envied Brenda for being beautiful and regal even when she was frustrated and dressed like a farmhand. This despite Charlotte usually feeling like a beached whale when she stood beside Brenda.

A short time later Charlotte and Dave were walking up the street to where the houses had been bulldozed toward the end of the point. Charlotte was being pulled along by both Sam and Rocket on their leashes and Burch was doing what he could to keep up. For a zaftig woman, Charlotte could move out real well. Of course the two dogs didn't usually give her any other choice.

"It's a real shame about the devastation here," Burch said as they approached the abandoned construction area. "That's the downside to closing down the plans for an illegal mob casino here. The cottages are already collapsed and the economy of the town is going to be hit hard."

"We hope to alleviate that," Charlotte said.

"We? I've been talking with a lot of the townspeople, and most of them are in a panic and not acting like they'll be much help in a recovery."

"Brenda and I have a plan—well, Brenda does. I'll have to think of something else if her plan doesn't pan out. It was a lovely village and can be so again. We can't just not get it back on its feet."

They were approaching the area. The last house standing on the right, against the river, was Charlotte's own cottage.

"Looks pretty desolate," Burch said. "Maybe the cottages can be rebuilt, though, once the ownership of the land is settled."

"Do you know anything about that—the status of the land ownership?"

"I assume it's still owned by whatever cutout company the mobsters used."

"But do you think it will be held in limbo as some sort of evidence?"

"I doubt it. We have criminal cases ongoing on the bodies that were dug up around here from when the mob used the area as a body dump—and the investigation of the deaths of your neighbors, the Wellses too—but the land itself? No, I think the mob backed out before anything criminal went down concerning the land. My guess is that whatever Realtor was handling the land sales would know."

"She's my Realtor too. I'll give her a call. But I didn't haul you out here for anything concerning my own cottage. The one I want to show you is across the street and up one collapsed house from mine. That's got . . . land's, Rocket, we're coming. You're really chomping at the bit this morning."

And indeed Rocket was huffing and pulling at the leash, anxious to get across the street. Charlotte didn't know the dog got that excited about anything other than a visit to the B&B across the street from Brenda's house. For some reason Rocket adored the Vales who lived in and operated the B&B.

"Do you see what I mean, Dave?" Charlotte said as they walked around the collapsed house.

"You mean all of these holes, like someone was digging for something?"

"Yes, it's probably not a police matter at all. But last evening I walked the dogs down here and there was someone back of this house digging. The dogs and I came to investigate and whoever it was slinked off into the woods behind the house. Someone seems to be looking for something here."

"And you're wondering what they're looking for?"

"I'm wondering more who it is—whether it's Ida Smith. Whether she hasn't left Hopewell at all. And Brenda's car going missing.

That could be Ida Smith too. She's done some carjacking in her day that we know of. I'm just worried about whether she's still here. If she murdered her cousin, she isn't beyond being a threat to others in the town."

"OK, I can see your worry—and can share it. We'll step up patrols around here."

* * * *

When Charlotte and the dogs returned to the house, Brenda was meeting with her financial manager, Frank Edmunds. Brenda had invited Charlotte to sit in on the meeting, but Charlotte didn't want to be in the position to influence Brenda in any way concerning what she did with what the taxes would leave her from the lottery money and she had a town council meeting to conduct at the community center later that afternoon, so she left Sam and Rocket with Bea in the kitchen and went out and pulled her car out of the garage. She had seen when Brenda came back from the store the previous evening that she hadn't gotten gas.

"I would have filled the tank," Brenda had said. "But I couldn't figure how to get the gas tank open." As Brenda drove a classic car she had no concept of a gas cap open button in the passenger compartment by the driver's seat.

Charlotte decided to fill the Escape and then to drive all of the streets—there being only a few of them—of the community before meeting with the town council. She knew it wasn't going to be a happy meeting. It was too bad, she thought, that she couldn't just put it off until after Brenda had some good news about revitalizing the community.

Jason William's garage was the far end of Penn Street from where the street started coming out of River Street beside the Vales' B&B, across the street from Brenda and Charlotte's house. The start of Penn Street was residential down to the Episcopal church, with the rectory beside it, and then there were only a few more houses leading into the village's small industrial area. The town's only gas station and garage was located just before the entrance into the industrial area.

As she drove, Charlotte thought about Ida Smith, who she was afraid might still be lurking around the town. Ida Smith had been the target of one of Charlotte's last FBI investigations. She had been implicated in a series of robberies that extended across state lines, which is what had brought the FBI into the investigation, and that had concluded with the murder of an old woman who had surprised the robbers by being home when she wasn't expected to be there. It was her regular hair appointment day, but she hadn't felt well and had canceled her appointment. Ida had eluded capture and had become the subject of a manhunt.

When Charlotte retired to Hopewell, she was surprised to find a woman, Edith Smith, living there, at Clagett's farm, who looked remarkably like the elusive Ida and then, when robberies occurred in Hopewell. Brenda, who had been employing Edith Smith as a part-time domestic, had been robbed. When it was discovered that Ida and Edith were nearly identical cousins, Charlotte and the sheriff's department concluded that Ida had stolen Edith's identity. Subsequently a body had been found in the farm's well, which could be either one of the women, but, having followed the case for years, Charlotte bet that the woman in the well was Edith and the woman on the lam was Ida, pretending to be Edith. While Brenda and Charlotte were in Florida working on a movie, this had been confirmed.

In passing down Penn Street, Charlotte saw evidence of an anticipation that was not going to be fulfilled unless something drastic happened. The façade of the Episcopal church had been taken off and the opening was under plastic sheeting. Plans had been to enlarge the sanctuary at the front. Across the street from that, an old Victorian house had been torn down and a small, modern-style Baptist church had been started. It looked like construction had been suspended, though. And in the last house before the gas station, a florist shop, with new glass display windows, had moved into the first story of another Victorian-style house. Even the gas station was showing signs of wanting to enlarge, but no longer sure it could. A bay extension had been started and concrete had been laid for another bank of gas pumps. What had been a small automotive parts storefront was being bumped out to accommodate a more extensive convenience store.

As soon as Charlotte drove up to the pumps, a young man of nineteen or twenty came out of the bay where a car had been up on the rack. He was cleaning his hands with a rag, and Charlotte surmised he had been changing the oil in the car. Charlotte couldn't remember ever having seen him before, and the village was small enough for her to recognize everyone who belonged here.

She was out of the Escape and pulling the gas nozzle out of its tray before the young man reached her. He was wearing jeans and a T-shirt, which were about as presentable as they could be for someone working with automobile oil, and he was trim, good looking, and his reddish-blond hair was buzz-cut short.

"Can I help you?" he asked as he approached. "I can get that for you."

"Thanks, I think I can pump it myself," Charlotte answered.

"Mr. Williams, he says I should pump unless the customer insists otherwise. No extra charge, of course."

"Very well, then, Just fill it until the machine pings, please. It will overflow quickly after that. I've already run the credit card."

"OK." He took the gas nozzle from Charlotte and she stood aside while he inserted it into her gas tank. "I'm Billy, by the way. Billy Zirkel."

"Nice to meet you, Billy. Do you work here now?"

"Yes. Well, I don't know for how long. Mr. Williams, he hired me when he thought there'd be a big buildup in town. Said he'd need the extra help. Now, I don't know."

"He may need you yet," Charlotte said, not wanting anything to be assumed too soon. "Is Jason around?"

"Mr. Williams? No. Not today. He's gone into Easton."

"Oh. We're having a town council meeting today. He's on it; I was checking on whether he'd attend the meeting. I'm Charlotte Diamond, by the way."

"Ah, yes, Mr. Williams told me about you. The town's mayor."

"More the pity, yes. Could you tell Jason to call me when he's back in town?"

"Yes, ma'am. There, the tank is filled now."

From Penn Street, Charlotte drove back out to River Street and turned left and then left again onto Main Street, where most of the businesses were. There had been so much construction and updating going on on Main Street that Charlotte had to stop the car and walk the

39

three blocks of the business area to check it all out. Nearly every business had been sprucing itself up or enlarging its showrooms. Seeing the beauty salon that had expanded sideways to take up what had been an alley and the new barber's chairs covered in plastic at the back of Walt Miller's shop, where the wall back there had been knocked out to add more barbers' stations made Charlotte remember the irate cell phone calls she had gotten from townspeople during the Atlanta layover when she and Brenda were flying back from Florida. Mary Miller, the town clerk, had been the most irate. Her problem was twofold. Not only were town revenues likely to decline with the destruction of the houses and departure of their residents but her own business, the village's beauty salon, and her husband's, the barber shop, were likely to go into the red for partial renovations that weren't going to result in added business.

Charlotte had no trouble seeing what the town's problem was, which had been caused by its business leaders trying to get a march on something that hadn't happened. It was their own fault, of course, but saying that to any of them wouldn't help the problem. Charlotte certainly wished for Brenda's plans to come through.

Someone had started four new houses at the very end of Spring Street and a building that looked like it would include four apartments in two stories, but there was no work being done on them when Charlotte reached the end of the road in the Escape. If Brenda's retirement complex went in, these would probably still be needed for staff members there, Charlotte thought. But, if not, Charlotte couldn't think of a need for eight more residential units in the town. She parked at the side of the street, pulled out her cell phone, and rang the Realtor, Scooter Wilson.

"Oh, hello, Charlotte," Scooter said tentatively on the other end of the call. She and Charlotte hadn't been on the best of terms since Scooter was handling the mobsters' end of the land acquisitions on the point and trying to handle the sale of Charlotte's cottage to them as well, while somewhat understandably giving more favorable service to the mobsters than to Charlotte. Charlotte didn't fault the woman for being careful with the gangsters; she faulted her for not revealing the depth of her involvement to Charlotte to give Charlotte the opportunity to move her listing to someone only looking out for Charlotte's interests. Of course Charlotte had run hot and cold on wanting to sell, which she acknowledged probably wasn't favorably seen by the Realtor.

"The sheriff's department told me that you could tell me where the land ownership and availability of the casino project stands, Scooter."

"Are you asking as mayor or because you either want to add your land to it or buy some of the land, Charlotte?"

"Yes to all of the above. Can the land be bought?"

"Yes. There are no encumbrances. Are you indicating that you might be willing to sell your cottage and land now?"

"Yes, but, if so, it would be as a private sale. I have a possible buyer and the buyer might be interested in buying all the rest of it too— if the price is right. I would let you handle the paperwork on my sale, though."

Scooter suddenly became at least marginally friendly. A fee for handling the paperwork was better than a client dragging her feet on selling to going to another Realtor altogether.

Charlotte used the opening to ask the second question she'd wanted to ask, the first being if the land even could be bought at this point. "Can you tell me who originally owned the three cottages across the street from mine—the ones that had been rentals and have been knocked down?" Charlotte wanted to know who to contact about why someone would be digging around that middle home.

"The shell company that bought the rest of the land."

"I mean before that. Were they owned by three different people, or one person? And who?"

Suddenly Scooter clammed up. "That's really not relevant to the sale of that land anymore. I'm not sure if I even remember."

"You did handle the sale on those properties, didn't you?"

"I'll have to check my records."

"OK, I'll talk to you later, after you've checked," Charlotte said. Maybe when I help serve the court order to make you tell me what I want to know, she continued in her thoughts.

When she got back to the house, Brenda was just winding up her meeting with Edmunds. The dogs were whining to get out, so Charlotte took them for a short walk, ending at the B&B across the street, where the Vales had been collecting Brenda and her newspapers and mail.

As Todd Vale met her at the door and opened the screen door, Rocket wiggled through and, with a woof, was off searching the downstairs.

"Rocket!" Charlotte called out. "Sorry, Todd, I don't know what he's up to."

"That's fine," Todd said with a smile. "Come on in and I'll get your mail and papers for you." Todd was the Vale Charlotte got along well with. Joyce, his wife, had inherited the big house. She had lived there as a girl when she was a Purcell. She'd gone off to college and married Todd. They'd lived in the big city where Todd had headed up the fraud unit of an international-level insurance agency and Joyce had been a senior book editor at a mainstream New York publishing house. They had retired here and opened the old family home as a B&B. Todd was the town's vice mayor and he and Charlotte got along just fine. It was not quite so with Joyce, however, since Charlotte had caused the arrest of Joyce's out-of-wedlock daughter the previous year.

But it was in the kitchen, where Joyce was, and after Charlotte had tied Sam's leash to a rattan rocker on the front porch, where Charlotte ran Rocket to ground. The dog was all over Joyce. Rocket and Joyce had a mutual affection that Joyce no longer was able to extend to Charlotte.

Pulling Rocket out of the kitchen with a minimal exchange of false pleasantries with Joyce, Charlotte stopped to talk to Todd briefly in the parlor.

"Will you be able to make the meeting this afternoon?" she asked Todd.

"Yes, I'll be there. I hope you'll have your armor on."

"Yeah, I can see why. I've just done a drive by of the village. A lot of overextension there, it seems. It's really their own fault. You haven't invested in premature anticipation, have you, Todd?"

"Not on your life. Joyce is the original Scrooge when it comes to shelling out money without a guaranteed return. But that doesn't matter much. We depend on tourists who want to come here. If the village looks like a war zone, they won't want to come here."

"I don't know who will be at the meeting," Charlotte said. "I've been to the gas station and Jason Williams is out of town."

"Oh, I think most will be there. Other than Jason and Grady Tarbell. Grady has classes to teach at Washington College and Jason is in Easton trying to make a new deal on the garage mortgage. He could lose it. And we could lose our only gas station. It could get real bad here in town. The Sheetz up on Route 50 is a bit far to go when you need gas, and you can't keep gas costs down if you have to use a gallon to get to the station and back."

Charlotte thought about that on her way back across the street. Frank Edmunds was getting in his car and Brenda was standing at the curb waiving him off. She was smiling, which Charlotte took as a hopeful sign. Charlotte walked up to her and turned to add her good-bye wave to Frank. The dogs happily settled down at their feet.

"So, how did it go?" Charlotte asked.

"I can do it if we start slow and maybe attract some more investment. David has already pledged some money, finally being resolved to be one of the first residents." She was referring here to her perpetual leading man in the movies, whose health, both physical and mental, was deteriorating quickly as had been evident when he was unable to fulfill his role in the movie shot in Florida in his usual flawless manner.

"The government will take a big chunk of the lottery money," Brenda continued, "but there will be some $60 million left over, and I have other funds of my own I can tap if I need to. The main building and maybe twenty residents is what we can start with. I have a list of some forty former movie folks who can be invited to come here, at the project's expense. We should be able to get twenty out of that."

"Forty former movie folks you know who need someone to cover their retirement home expenses? Movie folks?"

"Most movie people aren't that careful with their money. A lot of them end up destitute. Those are the ones I want to help."

"So that will be your selection criteria—destitute movie old folks?"

"One criteria, yes. Now we'll have to see about whether I can get the land."

"Yes, you can, if we don't let the sellers' hopes get up on what they can ask for. I called the Realtor, Scooter Wilson. The land's available."

"I'm delighted to hear that. It's a go then."

"Not as delighted to hear about it as I am. I now may not be torn limb from limb at the town council meeting this afternoon."

* * * *

Mary Miller, wringing her hands and looking like she hadn't slept for days, met Charlotte at the door of the community center. "This is a disaster, Charlotte. What are we going to do?"

Don't you mean what am I going to do, Charlotte thought. But what she said was, "Let's go inside, Mary. I think it will all work out. Are the others here?"

"All but Jason and Grady. Grady, of course, never shows up, and why does he care anyway? He works for a college across state, he's not suffering this catastrophe."

"It doesn't have to be a catastrophe, Mary. Let's just—"

But Mary wasn't listening. "Jason's not here because he's at the bank in Easton trying to save his business. It'll be Walt and me there on Wednesday, trying to do the same with ours. You just don't know—"

"Yes, I do know, Mary. I've been all over the town. I've seen the suspended construction. Perhaps you people shouldn't have been so quick to . . . but no need for that now. Just don't go too far down the road with your banking plans. I'm sure we can find a way out of this. Let's go inside."

Charlotte needed to walk a narrow line here. She didn't want to reveal Brenda's plans yet, if for no other reason than not to encourage anyone to try to run the cost of the land up to their own benefit. If Brenda couldn't get the land at distress sale prices, she wouldn't have enough money to get a building built and outfitted and a staff started. And then Charlotte didn't know what they'd be able to do for the town. Even twenty more residents in the retirement village would mean enough additional residents to support the business construction she'd seen—as long as the business community kept their expansion under control.

Mary was still jabbering while Charlotte guided her into the multipurpose room that, as usual, had its walls decorated with artwork from the class that met in here twice a week. And as usual Todd Vale's paintings were the only ones that looked to be professional quality. Mary's looked just like she was acting now—an abstract mess.

Todd himself was sitting at one end of the long table on a folding metal chair and looking nearly as worried as all of the rest, because, when all was said and done, even though the Vales hadn't put on any expansion and their property was long paid for, they were in as much of a predicament as anyone else.

Two the other council members present were the town's two women characters, who, although always at each other's throats, played off of each other and couldn't perform apart half as well as in tandem.

46

"Been off getting a Florida tan while our ship sinks, Missy?" Bonny Levitt, the town's oldest village resident and the self-styled institutional memory, asked. This was as friendly a greeting as Charlotte could expect from the wheelchair-bound senior citizen, but Charlotte long ago had adjusted to Bonny. The woman wasn't known for her humor, except for that which passed as sarcasm. She had survived three husbands, and no one in town questioned what they'd all died of. She was, in reality, all bark, though, and would run into a burning building to save any of the town residents, including her nemesis.

"We'll have to see about keeping the ship afloat," Charlotte answered crisply. "And glad to see you too, Bonny. And you, as well, Hannah," Charlotte said as she turned to the even older woman on the other side of the table from Bonny. "If I haven't told you in the last thirty minutes what a godsend your niece, Bea, is to Brenda and me, Hannah, let me repeat it again."

Hannah Helgerson, who had been about to launch into a community disaster lament all her own, suddenly beamed at Charlotte. Charlotte had found the right combination to derail her complaint, although she had no idea why this would be as much a disaster for Hannah as it was for others in the town. Hannah had been retired from the bakery she'd owned on Main Street for decades and was comfortably ensconced in the bungalow on Spring Street that her family had owned for generations.

The principle bone of contention between Hannah and Bonny was that Hannah saw herself also as the longest-living resident and historical touchstone of the village—and with, perhaps, by extension, better reason to do so than Bonny did. She claimed that her grandfather had been the village's blacksmith before the age of the automobile and

47

her father was the local farrier after that. Local belief was that she'd never been out of the village herself in the eight decades she'd been on the earth.

"That Bea of yours can clean a house well enough," Bonny said, giving Hannah a superior look, "but when it comes to baking a cake, I could show her a thing or two."

That was exactly the right jab to set Hannah, the former bakery owner, off. The two of them went into a trading of jabs and baking secrets that gave Charlotte a moment to talk quietly with the last of the council members present, sitting at the table end facing Todd, the Episcopal minister, Don Dunkel.

"Hannah looked as concerned as the rest when I came in, Don? Why is she so concerned?"

"She's a Baptist, you know," Dunkel said. "Been talking for years, don't you know, about having to worship at home because she couldn't step a foot in a high church such as mine."

"Ah, yes, I remember now," Charlotte said. "And that's a worry because?"

"She is the one backing the Baptist church being built across from mine. Have you seen it? They tore down the old Stilton house to put it up and have just gotten a start on it. Completely out of character of the neighborhood, of course. Rather like the Baptists, if you ask me. That applies to Hannah's concern because much of the money behind that is hers."

"I see. Well, we'll have to see about that. Thanks for telling me. Now, everyone, if we can come to order," she said in a louder voice. "Bonny and Hannah . . . please. I won't keep you long today, I just wanted to establish that I'm home and back in harness—and that I ask that you help to get everyone calmed down in the village. I know we can work this issue out. In fact, there is a possibility of something that will, I'm sure, satisfy everyone—as long as the building plans around here don't get any more ambitious than they have already."

"What do you mean, Charlotte?" Todd asked. "Does this mean that you know of someone else who is going to move in and develop the land?"

"There's a possibility, yes. But it's a delicate matter. I don't want to get into discussing it at this point. It's much too early. But if we can just get everyone to calm down and not do anything rash for a couple of weeks—"

"Does this mean that Joyce is gonna buy back those three rental properties of hers across the street from you, Charlotte?" Bonny asked. She turned to Todd Vale. "Your wife gonna buy those back and build cottages again? The old ones were gettin' so ratty that I thought they might just fall over before the bulldozers could get to them, anyway."

Todd was looking perplexed and started flapping his jaw.

Charlotte wasn't much less surprised. "Joyce Vale owned those houses?" she asked the assembled council members.

"Course she did," Hannah answered. "Everyone knows that. Her daddy had them before she did. Built them houses right after the big war. '46 or '47."

"T'weren't that war, Hannah," Bonnie broke in—as she always did in circumstances like this. "'T'was the Korean War, in the early fifties, and Joyce's daddy didn't always own them all. That one there in the middle he sold once and then bought back when that husband of a bank teller what owned it, Mr. Toms, disappeared."

"Their name was Thompson," Hannah said indignantly, "and that Thompson man was the banker."

"No t'weren't," Bonny overrode here. "It was the Toms, and she t'were the one who was a bank teller. She were the one goin' to prison for stealing that money they never got back. Hey, you just admitted that Joyce's daddy didn't always own all them houses." Rare clear triumph flowed across Bonny's face.

Hannah turned away and talked directly to Charlotte—red faced and determined to move away from her at least partial defeat. "There was always talk of her stealings being buried around that house somewheres. I'm sure I mentioned that to you, Charlotte. And I'm sure that, if you check, the name of the family was Thompson."

And now that she'd been reminded, Charlotte did recall hearing the story of a bank robbery connected to one of those houses. She was still nonplussed at hearing that the houses had been Joyce's, though.

"Always a strange house that, you know," Hannah continued, taking a side look at Bonny to ensure that she wasn't going to try to get back into the conversation to rub in that Hannah had forgotten that one of the houses had belonged to someone other than Joyce's father for a while. "Haunted some say. Some say that Mr. Thompson didn't just disappear—that his wife did him in and buried him somewhere hereabouts and that he keeps coming back to the house. In fact, his ghost has been pretty active lately. Several have talked about him roaming around near that house wreckage. Probably all angry the area's been bulldozed."

"Ain't no ghosts about, Hannah. You were always so superstitious. Guess it's the Baptist in you." Bonny had gone back on the attack. "No ghost of no Mr. Toms there at that house either. It's just swamp gas. Always has been. Comin' off that salt water holdin' pond behind the houses."

"That's most likely where Mr. Thompson's body is sunk," Hannah persisted. "Wasn't given a proper ground burial and roams around forever."

"No, Joyce hasn't bought those properties back," Todd Vale said in a voice that boomed out over Bonny and Hannah's game, which was leaving both of them glowing with pleasure. "At least she hasn't said anything to me about buying the houses back."

Now that Charlotte thought about it, she may have known that the houses belonged to Joyce Vale. Maybe her memory was going, she thought, with a bit of worry despite the minor war going on around her. She'd always been able to rely on a nearly photographic memory. Evan Worthington wanted her to come back and work as a consultant in the Annapolis FBI office, and she'd been thinking of doing so. Maybe she shouldn't even entertain that idea anymore. Maybe she was losing her memory. She hadn't remembered the story about the buried treasure at that middle house, either. That must be what whoever was digging around there at night was looking for. Would Ida Smith have heard about that legend while she was pretending to be Edith and moving around the village? Charlotte couldn't see why not.

"OK, I think we've met long enough for today," she declared in a loud voice. "I just wanted to touch base and ask you all to try to help calm the situation down. Can you do that?" It seemed an idiotic question, because they couldn't seem to even calm themselves down.

She looked around the table—mostly to blank faces. Well, it was the best she could do for now.

She walked out of the community center with Don Dunkel, who stopped abruptly on the steps outside the door.

"That's peculiar," he said.

"What is, Don?" Charlotte asked.

"I could have sworn I'd driven over from the church. I was going to drive over to the Sheetz for milk and bread that Mary asked me to pick up. I'll be glad if . . . no, when . . . ," he said, giving Charlotte an encouraging look, ". . . Jason gets in that convenience store he planned to add to his gas station. I won't have to traipse all over the county for incidentals then. But I was sure I brought the car over here. Must be getting old. Sometimes I have no idea where I've put my memory."

"You and me both," Charlotte said.

"It must be over at the church. Not a long walk, thank goodness. I just don't remember having done it today."

"I need to get back home, too," Charlotte said, looking over her shoulder at the approaching whirlwind. Hannah and Bonny were walking up to her, with Hannah pushing Bonny's wheelchair and the two returning to one of their longest ever arguments—what year the street lights were put in on Main Street, lights that Charlotte didn't think had worked for decades. She'd have to look into how expensive it would be to get those activated. Elderly residents of a retirement community wouldn't want to be walking in areas that weren't well lit.

* * * *

"Yes, of course I knew that Joyce Vale had owned those rental cottages across the street from you, Charlotte. I assumed you knew that as well."

"Maybe I did," Charlotte said.

Brenda gave Charlotte a level stare. "You aren't on about forgetting things again, are you? We all forget things."

"I never did before recent months."

"Before you and I met, you mean?"

"No, of course not."

"Have you forgotten this?" Brenda asked as she leaned over where Charlotte was sitting on the couch, petting Sam's head with one hand while a sprawled Rocket warmed her feet, and gave Charlotte a kiss.

"No, I don't think I ever could forget that," Charlotte said.

"Then that's all that matters," Brenda said, as she retrieved a cup of steaming coffee from the tray she had put on the coffee table and handed it to Charlotte. She then went over to one of the wing chairs, folded her legs under her in the chair, and took a sip from her own cup. As always, Charlotte got the impression of a regal queen on her throne.

As always too, though, Charlotte, who no one would describe as a small woman, felt like a bull in the china shop in the formal rooms of Brenda's eighteenth-century mansion. The most breathtaking rooms in the house, in Charlotte's estimation, were the two-story entrance foyer with the domed ceiling, painted in a cream color, and the sweeping staircase with the plush maroon stair treads and the nearly square dining room with the Sheraton furniture, Oriental carpeting, and the chinoiserie blue and white, with green and red accent wall paper, which Brenda had confirmed was almost as old as the house. The living room, with its Chippendale furniture, wasn't much less intriguing and yet intimidating to Charlotte. Truth be known, she was much more comfortable in the family room off the kitchen at the back of the house, which was decorated in current comfortable.

But this was where Charlotte had found Brenda when she returned from the town council meeting.

Brenda, ever polite, had wanted to hear Charlotte's report on the council members' behavior—to let herself rant a bit about that—before talking more of her meeting with Frank Edmunds. But Charlotte didn't vent for very long. She wanted to hear more about the retirement home.

"It might be close financially to get started," Brenda said. "But we have to start somewhere. Frank says he knows an architect who will probably donate his work when he knows it's me. It appears he's an avid movie buff."

"Being a gorgeous queen of the movies does have its perks," Charlotte said.

"Charlotte," Brenda said, with a smile.

"No, I mean it, Brenda. If you want to maximize your resources on this, you're going to have to realize and appreciate the power you have to get people to donate their services and money just to be able to stand by you—and you're going to have grit your teeth and let them sign the checks."

"I suppose. What do you think the best approach on buying the land on the point is?"

"I don't think that either you or I should go directly to Scooter Wilson. Whoever buys it is going to have to go through her, and I think she needs to think that it's someone who could just as easily locate their project elsewhere. I think you should talk to Frank again on who best can do that. It's probably Frank himself."

"Agreed. I just thought you'd want to use Scooter."

"Not in this lifetime, if I can avoid it," replied Charlotte. "She tried screwing us all three ways from Sunday on the casino deal. I'd really like to return the favor."

"You'd said you'd perhaps be willing to sell your cottage to add to the estate. If you did, we wouldn't tear it down. We'd use it as the construction office and then as a guest cottage or for some other purpose after the main building was built. It would make a good information and visitor's center, I think."

"I've been thinking about that," Charlotte answered. "I'm not willing to sell the cottage."

Brenda was taken aback a bit, but she rallied and said, "Well, of course that's fine. We can—"

"I won't sell it to you, because I am going to toss it into the mix for free," Charlotte said.

"I couldn't . . . there's no need to . . ." Brenda was so surprised that she couldn't find the words.

"You are putting all of these resources of yours into the project. And I see no reason why I shouldn't chip in some of mine too."

"Why, Charlotte . . . I don't know—"

"It would be a step in a direction I've wanted to take—that we've both been dancing around for some time," Charlotte said. "I think we must seriously start thinking of being full partners and making the commitments that entails."

"The full commitments?" Brenda asked.

"Yes. I don't think we should rush into it, but I think we should start thinking about it."

"You mean now that Maryland has passed the same gender marriage laws?" Brenda asked in a small voice.

"Yes. So, you've thought about it too?"

"Yes, of course."

"And does it scare you?" Charlotte asked. It was almost a whisper.

"Certainly, as I'm sure it does you. But, yes, I want to consider it seriously . . . if you do."

"Of course I do. And adding in my property to this project is a start in that direction."

"I certainly won't turn the offer down. But you know that you can withdraw it any time you wish. We'll keep it so it can be easily separated off, and we won't tear down the cottage. It can be something of a gatehouse to the rest of the area."

"So, have you thought what we're going to name this movie folks' retirement complex you are planning to build?"

"Yes. I thought we'd name it Curtain Call."

"A theatrical name? How fitting. I'm not quite sure what it means, though."

"The first name that came into my mind was Final Curtain, but then I thought that was a hideous name to put on an end-of-life institution. Curtain Call seems so much more upbeat. In the stage theater, it's that last bow the cast takes as the applause swells and then dies down and the curtain is closed. Here, it could be a celebration of all that had gone on before in these people's lives."

"That sounds perfect," Charlotte said.

"You know what would be perfect to seal our new understanding?"

"Yes, I do. Come over here," Charlotte said, her voice a bit husky.

The next several moments were quite private ones between the two women on the couch. Even Sam and Rocket had the decency to go down on their bellies, put their snouts down on the Oriental rug, cover their muzzles with their paws, and look away.

But that didn't last long—certainly not as long as Brenda and Charlotte would have liked.

The heads of both dogs came up simultaneously, their ears pricked up, and they turned toward the foyer. They were at the door, barking—but friendly barks both—before the doorbell rang.

This gave Brenda and Charlotte enough time to compose themselves, rearrange their clothing, and move toward the foyer.

Standing out on the front porch was the Reverend Don Dunkel. He looked confused and more than a little bit worried.

"It's gone," he said in a distressed voice when Brenda had opened the door. "I couldn't find the Buick anywhere. I think my car has been stolen."

Chapter Three: Some Solutions

"Yes, I know about the reverend's car," Jason said to Charlotte. "I've been arranging a cheap rental for him until they find the Buick."

"And you know that Brenda Boynton's Jaguar's been stolen as well?" Charlotte asked.

"That too."

Charlotte drove over to the gas station on Penn Street the morning after Don Dunkel appeared on the doorstep to report that his Buick had gone missing. Brenda and Charlotte had ushered him into the house and Brenda gave him tea and sympathy while Charlotte summoned Deputy Dave Burch. Then they'd spent a couple of hours with Dave getting all of the paperwork filled out.

"This is getting to be a rather bad habit," Burch had said.

"It certainly makes the theft of Brenda's car look like something more than a random effort to get out of town," Charlotte added. This actually disturbed her, because she had been half hoping that it had been Ida Smith who had taken the car and who was half way across the country by now. She feared for Brenda and the other residents of the village if Ida was still in the area. The woman not only was capable of doing almost anything illegal—she'd actually done almost everything illegal.

As much as the theft of two cars in the same small village whetted Charlotte's appetite for investigation, early in the morning Charlotte left that with Burch and took up her mayoral duties. She and Brenda had already gotten word from Frank Edmunds that he'd quickly negotiated a favorable price on the land at the point. After Brenda called him while Don, Dave, and Charlotte were working on the theft reports, Edmunds had started working on the transaction right away. He said he figured Brenda would ask him to do the negotiations for the land sale. He had someone else in his firm actually contact the Realtor. And as cagey as Scooter Wilson seemed to be in talking up the property, Edmunds noted that she quite obviously wanted to unload it as quickly as possible. No doubt the mobsters who owned it wanted to get out from underneath police scrutiny concerning the property even if they had to do so at a loss.

Frank's colleague had called Scooter and expressed interest in several plots of acreage around the county for a small housing development. He'd made sure that the land at the point was the only plot Scooter had the commission on herself. He'd been very iffy on how much he was willing to pay, and Scooter had given him a good quote on the land Brenda wanted. They already had a contract on it.

Knowing that the project was a go, Charlotte felt she had to start contacting those in the business community to assure them that help was on the way—and, Charlotte hoped—to both keep them from doing anything foolish with refinancing and to keep them from getting overenthusiastic with further expansion. They already, as a group, had gone beyond what they should have expected in the way of new business from the resort, and a retirement home would bring less business locally than the casino resort would have. Part of keeping it all tamped down would be talking with the business owners separately rather than in an assembled "event."

She felt she needed to start with the gas station owner, Jason Williams, because, since he hadn't attended the town council meeting, she knew he'd already been to his bank in Easton to talk refinancing—or maybe even bankruptcy.

When Charlotte drove up to the gas station, the new attendant, Billy Zirkel, hurried out of one of the bays and headed for the pumps. Charlotte smiled and waved him away, though, and parked over by where the new pumps were going in instead.

"You don't need gas?" Billy asked as Charlotte climbed out of the Escape.

"No, thanks, Billy. It's still nearly fill. I came to talk to Mr. Williams. Is he here?"

"Yes, ma'am, he's in the office."

"My, you seem an eager employee, popping out as soon as I pulled in," Charlotte said.

"Got to get this job down pat. I've only been on it two weeks, and I want to show I can do a good job."

"Two weeks?" Charlotte asked with surprise. "I would have thought you were here for a month at least."

"No, ma'am. Hired just three weeks ago. And you know how jobs are now. I need to keep this one, if I can. It's been especially hard for me to find work I can do."

"Hmmm. Just three weeks. So, Jason is in the office, you say?"

"Yes, ma'am," Billy said. "If there's nothing I can do, I guess I'd best get back to Ms. Helgerson's car. I don't think I've ever seen a Cadillac that old—or at least one that old in that good a condition. And such low mileage. But they all need an oil change now and again, cars that old more than most."

"Yes, you go on . . . and thanks for coming out even if I didn't need you. Good service like that can't be taken for granted anymore. And I'm surprised Hannah has kept that car of hers. I don't think I've seen it out of her garage before now. I wasn't sure she even knew how to drive."

"I'm not sure either, ma'am," Billy answered as he started back to the bay where the Cadillac was raised on the rack. "I had to walk over to her place and bring it back."

Charlotte had gone into the office, where Jason Williams was sitting behind a desk. He stood as soon as she entered. Don Dunkel's car problem was the first thing they talked about. Charlotte then mentioned the town council meeting.

"Sorry you missed the meeting," Charlotte said.

"Had to go to the bank in Easton," Jason answered. "And going over the accounts today to see what I can save here, if anything. It's pretty depressing."

"Easton Bank and Trust?" Charlotte asked. "I've found them understanding."

"No. I've always been with Talbot's. I'm afraid they've become pretty impersonal. The assistant manager I saw seemed to be right out of college and not all that sympathetic. But too bad about Reverend Dunkel's car, though. He loved that Buick, and we kept it in great shape between us. I just hope that . . ."

"You hope what, Jason?"

"Well, I don't know if maybe Ms. Boynton's Jag and now the Buick going missing is maybe at least partially my fault. Maybe I didn't make the best decision."

"I'm not following."

"Well, that new man I hired. Bill Zirkel. I know it's probably nothing and I shouldn't even entertain the thought, but . . ."

"What thought, Jason? You've already started to say something. What about the young man?"

"I took a chance and thought I was doing the right thing for society. But I guess Sheriff Wainwright will be bringing it up eventually. Bill's from a half-way house. This job was part of getting him back into society. He's done some prison time."

"He has? Do you know what for?"

"Car theft. But the placement office told me it was just a joy ride incident with some friends of his. That they got drunk and were just acting up. But he was of age, and they tried to sell the car, so he was given some time for it. But I thought I was just helping someone get straight and back on the job again."

"And maybe you are. That may be all there is to it," Charlotte said. "Did you say that Sheriff Wainwright knows about the arrangement?" She was looking at Williams' facial expressions closely, and he indeed did look concerned about the possibilities.

"Yes. Haws helped with the arrangements. I told him what I needed and was looking for to help with a work release program, and he put me in touch with the right state agency."

"Well, don't worry about it or say anything to anyone else about it, Jason. If the sheriff knows about the arrangement, I'm sure he'll factor that into the car theft investigation. And don't feel guilty. Being open to hire someone being rehabilitated like that is an admirable civic action. If it goes awry, that's not your fault or responsibility."

"I suppose. I just hope it doesn't backfire. But was there something you came to see me about today?"

"Yes. I just wanted to suggest that you not move too fast on any refinancing or anything more drastic than that. I think we may have something developing that could save the day. But don't get any fancier with your expansion plans, please. I don't think we'll manage anything as grand as the casino resort plan was."

"So, you think there may be something brewing on developing that land?"

"Yes, but it's not sure. So, I'd just hold for now, if I were you."

Charlotte didn't know why she wasn't more forthcoming on Brenda's retirement community plans. She had intended to be when she'd come here. But this discussion about Billy Zirkel had sidetracked her and put her off her mission. And now she had other visits to make today.

As she drove back on Penn Street toward River Street, she saw that Deputy Burch's patrol car was parked in front of the rectory, so she pulled in and went looking for Dave and Don. She found them in the church sanctuary and talked with them briefly. Mary Miller came in with the flowers for the altar for Sunday and pulled Dunkel away to complain about something. This was the woman's major occupation in life, but in this instance it didn't irritate Charlotte because it gave her an opportunity to talk with Burch alone briefly.

"I know it's early, but do you have any leads on the car thefts yet?"

"There's a possibility over toward Ocean City. There are informer reports of a car ring over there taking in classic cars to reship down to Latin America. But beyond that, no, we don't have any leads yet."

"It's a rather delicate subject, but I've just been at Williams' garage and Jason confided in me that his new employee, Billy Zirkel, is on a prison work release program."

"Yes, he is," Dave answered. "Sheriff Wainwright helped Williams get him set up. The kid has to be at the half-way house whenever he's not on the job. He's got an old clunker he goes back and forth in, but since he was trained as an auto mechanic in prison, he should be able to keep the car running."

"He seems to be a nice young man," Charlotte said.

"Yes, he seems to be, but we've got him high on the watch list for this, if that's what you wanted to make sure of."

"He told me he was hired just three weeks ago."

"Yes, that's right," Dave answered. "Williams thought he'd need extra help when the resort casino opened. I don't know how long he can keep Zirkel on now, though."

Just then Mary Miller and Don Dunkel were returning to them, and that was all that was said on that topic.

"Mary, I was just coming to see you," Charlotte said. "Let me walk you out."

Mary Miller had been high on Charlotte's list to talk to about the retirement community plan. In addition to be the village's unofficial town crier, Mary was also its squeaky wheel, and she had been the most upset about the collapse of the casino resort plan both because of her own business and because of her responsibility for the village finances.

Charlotte told her just about everything she knew on where they were with new plans—far more than she'd told Jason yet. And she was happy to see the relief in Mary's eyes and the less burdened gait in her step as she went to her car.

Charlotte felt the best she had in days to be able to bring that sort of relief. She'd contact the other business folks as soon as possible—Mary Miller had agreed to keep what she'd been told to herself until Charlotte had been able to talk to the others, which didn't keep Charlotte from thinking that she needed to get to the rest as soon as possible. But at the moment, Charlotte decided she needed to make a trip to Easton, the biggest town of any size to the northeast of Hopewell toward Annapolis. Cambridge, to the southeast farther down the banks of the Choptank was actually larger than Easton and closer, but there was no civilization beyond it, so Hopewell residents found themselves gravitating to Easton more often. Charlotte hadn't seen the need to go there today before coming out into the community, but she did see the need now, if for no other reason than that was where Sheriff Wainwright kept his office and she wanted to consult with him and something that was nagging the deep recesses of her mind. In the event, though, she had to hold her thoughts and concerns, because Wainwright wasn't in his office when she checked both as she entered Easton and then right before she left.

* * * *

Charlotte couldn't say that it was the biggest yacht she'd ever seen, but it certainly looked gigantic lashed to the pier behind the house when she returned from her journey to Easton in the mid afternoon. It wasn't big in comparison to Brenda's mansion, but it certainly was big compared to Charlotte's own cottage farther up the street. And it was gigantic compared to the baby-blue Prius hybrid sedan sitting in the driveway.

Brenda met her at the front door, flanked by Sam and Rocket, who continued out onto the porch, tails wagging, to insist on a proper pet and head scratch greeting from Charlotte. "Do you like my new wheels?"

"Quite a change for you," Charlotte said.

"Frank had it delivered to me a few hours ago. It's on a short-term lease, hoping that the Jag will be recovered soon. But if I like it, I might switch over. I think I'll have to make a few economies to accommodate our retirement home project."

"Switch over?" Charlotte asked, giving Brenda her best skeptical expression.

"Well, add if they can recover the Jag," Brenda said, with a laugh. "You know me so well."

"You said 'our project,'" Charlotte said. "I like the sound of that."

"As do I," Brenda responded.

"I can see why you are economizing on cars," Charlotte went on, "if you've traded your Laser sailing boat in for that ocean liner parked out back."

"Ah, that's Douglas'. He sailed it down from St. Michaels."

"Douglas? St. Michaels? Was my trip to Easton long enough that I missed the whole second reel of this movie?"

"Douglas. Douglas Dolan. He's the architect Frank was telling us would be willing to work on the retirement community plans for free.

He works out of St. Michaels, and he says he goes by boat whenever he can."

"If I owned a yacht like that, I would sail it everywhere too," Charlotte said. "You say he's here?"

"Yes. And he's so enthusiastic; he says he has some rough plans to show us already. We were just about to—"

"That's fine. I'll get out of your hair while you meet with him. I'll take the dogs for a walk."

Both Sam and Rocket understood what she said, and they suddenly became quite frisky to vote their approval of this idea.

"Oh, no. We're partners in this now," Brenda said. "I want you to be as much in the discussions on the plans as I am."

"Maybe too late now," Charlotte said, "The dogs are listening. Look at how they have their ears perked up. They know there was a walk in the plans, and I'll have to take them now, even if only on a short one."

"That's quite all right. I'm having an enjoyable time getting acquainted with Tony. We'll just chit-chat until you get back."

Charlotte didn't much like the sound of that either. Brenda's eyes were flashing like they did when she was interacting with her perpetual leading man in films, David Runion, who she had pined after for decades only to finally discover he was far more interested in men than women, incredibly including Brenda, who nearly every man fell for. Charlotte was almost afraid to meet this Douglas Dolan, but she was more afraid of that gleam in Brenda's eye when she mentioned the architect.

She'd take the dogs on a walk, but it would be the world's shortest dog walk.

As they moved down the front path to the street, Sam and Rocket at a trot and Charlotte more at a trudge, Charlotte saw that Joyce Vale was weeding the flower beds at the B&B across the street. Joyce had turned an eye toward Charlotte, and Charlotte jauntily waved. But Joyce either didn't see her or pretended not to see her and Charlotte lowered her hand slowly.

She didn't know if Joyce ever would forgive her for discovering that her natural-borne daughter, one she had birthed out of wedlock after an unlikely coupling with Grady Tarbell when they both were teenagers, was a thief. Susan Purcell, who had come to the village as the director of the village arts center in the community center building, when Hopewell was unsuccessfully trying to become an artsy Mecca for this region of the state, hadn't revealed that she was Joyce's daughter, although some of the older residents knew that. She rented the cottage next to Charlotte's and proceeded to enter neighbor's homes and, using her knowledge of art, walk off with the more priceless family heirlooms she found. Charlotte had found her a secretive, moody woman, but she was as surprised as anyone to discover, first, that she was a thief, and, second, that she was Joyce Vale's daughter. But Susan had gotten in over her head with what she knew about a murder mystery Charlotte was investigating and managed to get herself killed before Charlotte could curtail the activities of the murderess. And for both outing Susan as a thief and not stopping her from being murdered, Joyce Vale blamed Charlotte.

Charlotte had tried—and still would try if Joyce let her—to be a friend to Joyce, but she found that Joyce had some of the same secretive and moody traits as her daughter had—and she seemed unable to view what had happened to her daughter, and why, objectively.

Sam and Rocket pulled Charlotte in the direction of the point, and Charlotte let them carry her along. They obviously wanted to do more than just exercise and relieve themselves. They pulled Charlotte toward the front door of Zenna's bakery in the community center building. Zenna saw them coming and met them at the door with a handful of pigs-in-the-blanket, little sausages wrapped in crescent rolls, which she placed on the bricks of the walk up to the bakery's door and Sam and Rocket had no trouble finding and inhaling.

"You shouldn't indulge them like that," Charlotte said.

"They were stale. I'd rather these honeys get them than the trashcan," Zenna said.

"Are you going to be here later this afternoon?" Charlotte asked. "I have something to discuss with you, but I have a meeting back at the house and I have to get these beasties home as well."

"Certainly. I feel like I'm here all the time," Zenna said.

As Charlotte turned to go back to the house, Billy Zirkel passed her driving Hannah Helgerson's old Cadillac. Charlotte had a sudden pang of concern that he was stealing it or taking it on more of a joy ride than checking out how it ran warranted, but then she realized that he was just returning it to Hannah's place after having serviced it. She berated herself for jumping to conclusions and then stopped and gave that a bit of thought. She usually was more objective than that; perhaps this was another indication that she had lost her edge. But then she had other claims to her attention. Having had the treat they obviously assumed they would get and that they deserved, Sam and Rocket were pulling Charlotte back toward the house.

The dogs seemed extremely anxious to be home again, and when Charlotte got there and saw Brenda and Douglas Dolan in close, laughing discussion in the living room of the mansion, Charlotte wondered if the dogs weren't just as sensitive to domestic danger as she was.

Just as Charlotte feared, Douglas Dolan was a handsome fellow, and beyond that, a hunk. And he was a hunk in the worst possible way. He wasn't some young man who Brenda could appreciate in the abstract and know that he was not to be toyed with. He was much the same age as Charlotte and Brenda were. And he had great silver gray hair that many women of this age would have paid big bucks for at the beauty parlor. He was trim and dapper looking in a casual way that screamed of good taste and money. And he had a smile and a laugh that brought out the same in Brenda. Charlotte didn't know of anyone but herself; Brenda's leading man, David Runion; or her heart-throb movie actor son, Tony Trice, who could get Brenda to smile this broadly.

The only man Charlotte could think of who was any more perfect on surface inspection was her own past flame and the current head of the FBI's Annapolis office, Evan Worthington. But as soon as that thought struck Charlotte, she tried to suppress it. And she rather thought that Brenda would choose this handsome yachtsman and architect over Evan anyway. Charlotte's worry was who else Brenda might ultimately choose him over.

She had walked in on them laughing and with their heads very close together over large sheets of paper that were spread out on the coffee table. Charlotte had started to enter the room but then thought better of it based on the intimacy she thought she could see between the pair. So, making a good deal of noise—with the help of barking dogs— she took Sam and Rocket back to commune with Bea Helgerson in the kitchen before she came back to the parlor, stopping just short of the door to practice which false smile she wanted to use, and then, after choosing one, plunging on into the room in her usual "body too big for the delicate furniture" style.

"Oh, there you are, Charlotte," Brenda called out. She had just come off of a round of her famous tinkling laughter, which earned her a good fifty-thousand-dollars more in her movie contracts. "Douglas here was so enthusiastic about his concept for the retirement complex that we couldn't wait. And I must admit that I'm as enthusiastic as he is. Oh, Douglas, this is my partner, Charlotte Diamond. Charlotte: our architect Douglas Dolan."

Charlotte had wished that Brenda had been a little less cryptic concerning what "partner" entailed, and within a half hour she was distressed to find out that she was no less enthusiastic about Douglas' concept for the complex than he and Brenda had been.

"I had been thinking of one main building for assisted living," Brenda said, her voice dripping with excitement, "with cottages dotted around the acreage Win Engleton had developed on the point for those in independent living, but Doug here has this entirely different concept. See these sketches. What do they look like to you?"

Oh, it was "Doug" already, Charlotte thought, with a bit of consternation. "They look like a line of attached Irish cottages."

"Yes, but . . . oh, you would never have seen them."

"Seen what?"

"This is just what the actors' studios on the back lot of the movie studio I filmed for looked like in the early days. The residents will feel right at home with this concept. It's amazing that Doug researched this so deeply already. He had already found out what our studio apartments looked like. And they will be similar inside too—a living

72

area, including a kitchenette, with a bedroom and bath off it. And the doors will be extra wide. The interior doors will be pocket doors so that the residents can't get trapped behind them or have trouble going through them if they're in a wheelchair or have a walker."

Of course Dougie had already researched this. From the way he was looking at Brenda, he had researched Brenda very well too and was lost to her. There was nothing peculiar about that, of course, nearly all men—except for the one Brenda had once really wanted—went gaga over her. But this one had researched her well. Frank Edmunds had said he was willing to donate his services to this. Charlotte could see now exactly why. He had designs on Brenda. And at the same moment that Charlotte thought of Douglas' designs, Brenda used the word, which brought Charlotte's attention back to the present.

"And the way Doug has designed this, there need not be a transition from independent living to assisted living. The residents should be able to remain in their original units to the end unless they needed an ICU unit. Look. There's the central dining and living facility and then three wings of connected cottages going off that in three directions. That will mean there will be seven residential cottage units in each wing, and one of the units half way down the wing will encompass a nurse's station, storage rooms, and a resident's lounge. Of course one wing will have to be set up for dementia and Alzheimer's patients."

"Of course," Charlotte agreed. She was thinking of the actor David Runion, who had shown signs of losing his facilities during their recent Florida movie shoot and who, Charlotte was sure, was the inspiration for this whole actors' retirement community idea. Runion was to be among the original residents and even was donating money to the cause.

"But the cottages open up to the outside, Brenda," Charlotte said, wanting to contribute some critical input, not wanting this seemingly perfect Douglas to come across as totally brilliant. "Is that practical? Making the residents and the staff workers come out into the elements to go anywhere."

"That's the brilliance of it, Charlotte. This view is just of the one side. The back of these units will be one long, wide hallway extending all the way down the wing, with gradual ramps to allow for the cottages to be on slightly different levels and prevent them from looking institutional. And the beauty of this is that it's built for expansion. For now, the cottage rooms will come off on only one side of the wing, but when we are able to expand, we can double the units by building them off the other side of the wings as well. And we can extend the wings for even more units. Isn't that beautiful? Isn't that brilliant?" She was looking admiringly at Douglas, who was returning a look that Charlotte couldn't believe Brenda didn't see the worship in.

"Yes, brilliant. Beautiful," she answered, hoping her voice didn't sound too flat. She looked carefully at the sketches, trying her best to find the flaw, but she was saved the embarrassment of not being able to find any by the sound of the front doorbell chime and the dogs beginning to bark in muffled tones from the distant kitchen. At least she thought she had been saved, but, in fact, matters got more complex and distressing.

Brenda left Charlotte to smile weakly at Douglas Dolan as she went to answer the door. Charlotte would have given a bundle to have been the one to go answer the door, but Brenda was much more swift of movement. Charlotte didn't have time to lumber out of the wing chair she was dominating before Brenda's trim figure was at the door into the foyer.

"Look who I found," Brenda said when she returned.

Oh, my god, Charlotte thought, but what she did was dredge up a smile and greet their visitor. "Hello, Evan," she said.

Standing in the doorway between the foyer and the parlor was Evan Worthington. He was looking a little sheepish when he saw that there was another man here, and meekly handed over the bouquet of roses and box of chocolates he was carrying to Brenda. "These are for you ladies," he said. "A welcome home present. You weren't coming to see me, so I decided to come to see you."

He made it sound like the gifts were for both of them and that he was referring to both of them not having come to see him, but Evan had been on a campaign to get back together with Charlotte for some time, so she wasn't fooled what his intent was. For a savvy FBI senior agent, he always had been clichéd about his courting gifts. But his corniness in gifts was exactly one of the key aspects of him that Charlotte found endearing.

"Please, come in, Evan. We were just looking over the sketches for a concept for the retirement community Charlotte and I are planning to build here in Hopewell with our architect here, Douglas Dolan. Doug, this is a former colleague of Charlotte's from the FBI, Evan Worthington. Can I get you something to drink, Evan? And you too, Doug? You'll have to excuse me. I was so excited by what you had to show me that I didn't even think of offering it before."

"The drinks tray is right over there, Brenda," Charlotte said. "Someone must have thought about drinks."

"Why, I'll bet that was Bea. She is so efficient that it scares me sometimes."

"I really don't want to intrude," Evan said. He looked confused. He had known nothing about any retirement community plans.

"Of course you're not intruding, Evan," Brenda said. "You've come all the way from Annapolis to see us. And I know you don't know what we're talking about concerning plans for a retirement community here. We'd be delighted to include you in our discussions on that, wouldn't we, Charlotte?"

"Umm. Yes, of course we would." Charlotte was in a panic. There were entirely too many handsome men in this room obviously interested in the wrong women.

"May I suggest that we take our drinks down to my boat?" Douglas said. "We could even go out on the river for a while."

"That's quite a yacht you have there, Douglas," Evan said, obviously genuinely interested in it. "It looks like it's a classic from the thirties."

"Yes it is. It's a 1935 Mathias eighty-five footer. I dock it at St. Michaels. I live on it most of the time."

"I'd love to have a tour," Brenda said.

"And you must have a sail as well," Douglas responded. "What about now? The weather is ideal today for a sail on the river and maybe even out into the Chesapeake Bay."

"It's close enough to supper that we could have Bea put something together and eat dinner on the yacht—the four of us. Wouldn't that be fun, Charlotte?" Brenda obviously was delighted by Douglas' proposal.

"Yes, delightful," Charlotte answered, thinking anything but delightful. "But maybe Bea won't have enough time to prepare something. I'll just go ask."

When she hit the door of the kitchen, she found Bea humming and putting together enough shrimp salad to feed a small army.

"I heard," she said. "There will be plenty for you all to have dinner on the boat."

This was perhaps the first time that Charlotte cursed Bea's efficiency under her breath. She was in a panic. This was all just too much for her—and not because she wouldn't enjoy herself or didn't ever want to see Evan again. But more because she was still conflicted about what she wanted and she feared that Brenda was too. And those two men were just too enticing. She had to think of something to take a breather from this so she could regroup for supper on the yacht.

She stopped in the hall to regather her wits, put on a smile, and came back into the parlor. "Bea's her usually efficient self," she said. "If you like shrimp salad, we have a dinner for the boat."

Both of the men piped up declaring their love for shrimp. Rats, Charlotte thought.

Sighing, she bowed to the inevitable. "But you'll have to start with the drinks without me, I'm afraid. I do have one visit I have to make today on town business. Something I can't put off."

"That's fine," Douglas said. "I think you can find the boat when you're ready to join us."

"I think the whole town knows where that boat is," Charlotte said, which brought a jolly laugh all around. Everyone quite evidently was comfortable—everyone except Charlotte—and she was damned if she'd admit she wasn't.

"May I take some of those sketches with me, Douglas?" she asked. "It will help me in the meeting I'm going to."

"Yes, of course," he said. But he already had returned his full attention to Brenda.

Charlotte had not really lied. She had fully planned to go to Zenna's bakery today and tell her about the plans for the retirement community.

"It's a wonderful idea," Zenna said. She was sitting at a table in the bakery with Charlotte, and her helper, Evonne Clagett was fluttering around, making sure they had tea and coffee and anything else they could possibly want.

"I'm glad you approve," Charlotte said, happy to see the relief that flooded Zenna's face. "You can go on with your plans to move to Main Street in a bigger facility now. But it would be wise not to get too ambitious with it. The home won't be up and running for some months, probably almost a year, and then it will mainly be the staff members who are added to the business community's clientele."

"I understand. I haven't put that much into the expansion yet and I may just let the lease on Main Street go when it's due until I can gauge how much the business will grow. I'm just relieved for the others in town."

"And so am I," Charlotte said.

"Excuse me, I couldn't help but overhear that a retirement community is going in here on the point." Evonne Clagett was standing over them, holding a teapot.

"That's right," Charlotte answered. "It will be for retired movie people Brenda has worked with."

"They'll be hiring staff then, I suppose."

"Yes, certainly," Charlotte answered.

"Then I'd be might grateful if you let me know when the hiring starts," Evonne said. "That's what I did before Kevin and I moved back to his old farm. I was the assistant director of a nursing home in Bowie."

Charlotte looked quizzically at Zenna.

"I think it would be wonderful if Evonne got a good job there," she said. "She's much too good a worker to be working here part time and it probably now will be some time before I really need extra hands. She and I have been talking about finding a better position for her."

"Well, then, I'd be happy to let you know about hiring when we get to that stage," Charlotte told Evonne. "There's no question of your capabilities."

* * * *

Charlotte was miserable all evening. She was having a ball socializing with Brenda and these men on the yacht—as they all appeared to be having. The shrimp salad was out of this world, and the cruise on the Choptank River in the luxury eighty-five-foot yacht made her feel like visiting royalty.

She was absolutely miserable she was having such a good time.

At one point in the evening, even though she was keeping an eye on what Brenda and Douglas were in deep conversation about, she found that she and Evan were alone in conversation.

Naturally—as she managed to maneuver matters—they engaged in shop talk. After Evan had brought her up to speed on the recent lives of the personnel she had known in the Annapolis office and even about some of the major cases they were following—with him obviously trying to entice her to develop an interest in the cases and thus accept his oft-proffered request that she come back and consult with the office—Charlotte brought up a concern of her own.

"Evan, do you remember a case the office had—it was one of my last cases—of Ida Smith?"

"I don't remember much about the case before she was suspected of murdering her sister here in Hopewell. I think her earlier exploits were before my time in Annapolis. Why do you ask?"

"Has she been apprehended while Brenda and I were in Florida?"

"Not that I know of. But I could check on the status of the case for you, if you'd like."

"Could you please? I'm afraid there's a possibility that she might not have left the area. We have a few strange happenings going on in town, and I feel responsible to follow up, both because I'm mayor and because I worry for Brenda, especially now that she has all of this lottery money."

"Yes, of course. Do you want to see the file we have?"

"I think I do, yes. I worked the case, but I keep thinking there's something I've overlooked—or no longer clearly remember. I have a nagging feeling there's something about names I should be aware of. Like Ida Smith was operating under another name earlier that should ring a bell with me but doesn't."

"I'll have a copy of the file brought to you tomorrow—unless you'd prefer coming into Annapolis for it. We could have lunch."

"I don't think I can leave the village just now, Evan. I know it's an imposition, but it would be a great favor to me if I could receive the file here."

"There's nothing more I'd like to do for you than a great favor," he said.

Charlotte had to look away. The look in his eyes was too revealing for her to endure. And that's why she couldn't come in to Annapolis to see him in the office—or to go to lunch with him. She simply couldn't trust herself to be alone with him.

They did return to land before midnight without the situation getting entirely out of hand in Charlotte's eyes, and the men did eventually both leave.

Charlotte and Brenda hadn't been in bed for more than an hour, though, when the doorbell rang. When Charlotte went to an upstairs window, she saw Dave Burch's cruiser parked out front. The lights were ablaze in the B&B across the street too, which was a surprise to her.

She went down and let Dave in.

"Sorry to disturb you this late at night, but I knew you'd want to know that we caught the nighttime digger up the road at that collapsed cottage across the street from yours—and it wasn't any ghost."

"Yes, of course we want to know," Brenda said as, dressed in an elegant robe, she reached the bottom of the stairs in the foyer.

"It was a treasure hunter all right, set off by the legend of that bank clerk and a bank robbery in the fifties," Dave said.

"Who?" Charlotte asked, going directly for the punch line.

"Your neighbor across the street, Joyce Vale."

"Joyce?" Brenda and Charlotte exclaimed in unison.

"Yep. She at first claimed the land was hers to dig if she wanted. When I asked her why she was doing it in the dark at night, though, she got real defensive. She knows as well as anyone would that she was trying to avoid paying any taxes on it or having it confiscated if she did find something."

"But, the land isn't hers. It's Brenda's, or will be as soon as we can arrange settlement, and it was someone else's before that since Joyce owned it."

"Now, Charlotte," Brenda said.

"I know you were raised with Joyce and you went to school with her, but you've got to admit she has a nasty edge to her," Charlotte said.

Brenda laughed at that. "She did at school too," she said.

"Yep, I called her on the land ownership question. But I told her we'd just forget it if she'd just stop it. I hope that's OK."

"Yes, of course," Brenda said quickly, not giving Charlotte a chance to voice another choice.

"She asked me not to tell anyone," Burch said. "But by then I'd put a trace through on the land and Ms. Boynton's financial man came up as the purchaser—and he told me he'd bought it for Ms. Boynton. So I told Mrs. Vale I had to at least tell her—but I wouldn't nose it around and I didn't think Ms. Boynton would either."

"No, of course not," Brenda answered.

"Anyhow, she would know I told you because here I am, just across the street from her place. But that's not the only reason I thought you'd want to know tonight."

"Oh?" Charlotte said, her ear perking up. She almost laughed, though, because both Sam and Rocket were standing between Brenda and her in the foyer and what Burch said had made their ears go up as well. I certainly hope they don't think they're getting a walk at this time of night, she thought.

"Mrs. Vale insists that she only started digging a few days ago—and then only because she noticed that someone else had been digging. She says most of the holes around that house were dug by someone else."

"Damn," Charlotte exclaimed.

"Charlotte!" Brenda said in mock disapproval. Charlotte just smiled, because Brenda was the more likely of the two to swear.

Acting like he hadn't even noticed, Burch said, "I guess if she's telling the truth, that means we are right back where we started from on the mysterious digger in that yard."

"Yes, it sounds very much like that's true," Charlotte agreed. "So, thanks doubly for letting us know as soon as you could. We'll be on our guard."

Burch tipped his hat and headed for the foyer. "So, we will just continue our patrols of that area, at least for a while." And then he was gone.

Standing at the door, with the dogs panting happily between them, Brenda and Charlotte could see someone at one of the upstairs windows of the Vales' B&B. Neither one of them doubted that it was Joyce Vale, or that this incident wouldn't make her any less sour on her neighbors across the street.

Chapter Four: Chased Down

Charlotte hadn't slept well that night because of her feeling of guilt about asking someone from the Annapolis office to come all the way out here with a copy of the file on Ida Smith. Although she was a late riser now in retirement—although nowhere near as late in getting up as Brenda, ever the movie star, was, she groaned out of bed at 8:00 a.m. and padded into another room to call the Annapolis office. She asked for Margaret Fancel, who had been her assistant before Charlotte retired and who was Charlotte's "go to" person there when she didn't go straight to top and call Evan. She was too embarrassed to call Evan, and she still didn't want to get entangled in any intimate luncheon dates with him.

"Hello, Charlotte. How was Florida?"

"Mosquito infested, at least the part I was in."

"You'll have to tell me all about it. I am, of course, fascinated with mosquitoes. I see that I'm on the road this morning bringing you a copy of the Ida Smith file."

"Oh, good, you're the one who has it," Charlotte said. "Let me save you some trouble on that. It appears I'll be out your way this morning. How about rather than you driving all the way down here, that I meet you someplace in Annapolis for lunch and we can exchange the file then."

"Sure, that's fine with me. Any favorite place?"

"How about Carrol's Creek Café at the Eastgate section of the waterfront. I haven't been there in a while."

"That sounds good. Say noon? Shall I see who else—?"

"No one else, please, Margaret. I'd spend too long at the trough, and I don't really have the time or waistline to spare. Oh, and no need to tell Evan Worthington I'm coming in. It's a little embarrassing; I told him yesterday I couldn't come in and he did this big favor of agreeing to send the file to me here. And now I've had this change of plans."

"Well, OK, but if he sees me still in the office this morning—"

"Well, then, you can tell him I called and had a change of plans, but I have so much to talk with him about and don't have the time today. It would be best that he not know I was there for lunch. He might take it wrong."

"OK, I understand," Margaret said, and Charlotte was afraid that maybe that was exactly right—that Margaret would know that Charlotte was trying to duck Evan for reasons other than office ones.

When they met, they spent so much time catching up with each other's activities and those of mutual colleagues that it was only toward the end of lunch that the topic of Evan came up again.

"I'm glad you've been promoted up to agent, Margaret," Charlotte said. "You're good at it and a great benefit to the office."

"It's largely because of recommendations you made, Charlotte. And that of Evan Worthington, of course. He's a great boss—and a great guy too. I don't know why you are holding him at arm's length, Charlotte, not just in coming back to consult with us but also as a suitor. He's perfect in every way in that regard as far as I can see, and he clearly adores you."

"We had our innings, Evan and I," Charlotte answered. "But that is long over. He is perfect, yes. It's me who isn't perfect in every way, and we've tried it and it just didn't work out."

"I think you down rate yourself too much. I think you'd be quite a catch."

"For the right person, perhaps," Charlotte responded. "But, sorry—and I'm probably more sorry than you are—Evan just isn't the right catch for me."

Margaret sighed. "Well, at least you could come back as a consultant. We could use you. It seems like the aheader we go in this business the behinder we get."

"I'm not as sharp as I used to be," Charlotte answered, "I see evidence of that every day."

"Nonsense. From what I heard you wrapped up a spy ring down in Florida and solved a decades' old mystery. That doesn't sound like you've slowed down."

"But I have. And I think people like us—FBI agents responsible to the people—need to be able to recognize it when it happens. God, I'm older than the hills. It's time I slowed down. Yes, we got some mysteries solved down in Florida, but if I'd been quicker on the uptake, there would have been less tragedy before we did. And that's what I'm afraid is happening with this file." She picked up the Ida Smith file. "There's something about this that's really bothering me. Something I should have remembered or connected with something else—and that

I would have when I was on the job. And, speaking of that, I think it's time for me to get home and start poring over this file. Lunch is on me."

"Oh, no it's not."

"Oh, yes it is. I gave them my credit card when I came in, and they've already run it. It's what you get for meeting me at one of my favorite restaurants in Annapolis. They still know me here."

Charlotte was already hauling her bulk from behind the table and smiling at the waitresses she knew well and hadn't seen in several months. Margaret didn't continue the fight for the bill. She knew that Charlotte won any struggles she really wanted to win.

While she was driving back to Hopewell, Charlotte almost missed what broke one of their local mysteries wide open because she was so engrossed in thinking about her complex relationship with Evan. Normally she could have cleared the air—or at least cleared the decks—by telling him that she and Brenda were in a relationship. But he knew that already and didn't seem to care. He wasn't at all belligerent toward Brenda. They got along just fine. He just said he didn't think that Charlotte was sure enough for him to stop offering other possibilities—that she was attracted to one particular woman wasn't enough to make him give up.

What she almost missed was Hannah Helgerson's old Cadillac turning right from the Hopewell road onto Route 50 and gunning its way in the direction of Ocean City on the Atlantic coast. Although she couldn't get a good look at who was at the wheel, it looked like a man and it certainly was much too compact to be Hannah, who, everyone knew anyway—or had been led to assume—couldn't drive.

Instead of turning toward Hopewell, Charlotte began following the car—at a distance, letting other cars get between them often enough that whoever was driving the Cadillac wouldn't get suspicious that someone was following unless they were quite attentive. As she drove, she fished her cell phone out of the purse laying on her passenger seat and pressed the button for Deputy Dave Burch's cell phone, something she never would have done while driving if this didn't have all the markings of an emergency.

"Hi, Ms. Diamond. What's up?"

"Do you have any patrol cars out on 50 between the Hopewell exit and Ocean City?" she asked.

"Yeah, me. Why?"

"I just saw Hannah Helgerson's Cadillac zoom out onto the highway from Hopewell, headed for Ocean City. It's slowed down to the posted limit, though, like whoever is driving doesn't want to be stopped."

"I thought Hannah Helgerson didn't drive."

"Bingo. I can tell there's a man at the wheel. I just can't tell who it is."

"You're following the car? You're calling me on your cell phone and driving?"

"Are you driving, Dave?" Charlotte asked, "and talking to me on your cell phone?"

"Touché. But you know—"

"We don't have time for that, young man," Charlotte commanded in her FBI agent voice. "I suggest you call Hannah, if you can get her number, and ask her if she's letting anyone drive her car."

"Are you sure it's her car?"

"Do you know anyone else in the county who owns a late fifties lime green Cadillac convertible?"

"Touché again," he said, almost chortling this time. "I'll ring you back whether or not I can get hold of her. But you be careful now. I'm heading back from the Ocean City side. When I see it, I'll pull it over in any case."

"No, I suggest you don't do that, Dave. Check with Hannah. If she's loaned the car, I'll turn around. If not, I'll have another suggestion. In the meantime I suggest you pull off to the side, away from the highway but positioned so you can see what's coming from my side."

"Because I shouldn't drive and use the phone at the same time?" he asked, capable of making Charlotte think of that cute twinkle he had in his eye just from his tone of voice.

"No, so he doesn't see you and get spooked."

Mere minutes later, Burch called back. "Nope, she didn't give permission for anyone to drive her car and she's fit to be tied. I had to use dynamite to get her off the phone, telling her we thought we had the car in sight and would have it back to her quickly. Now, I'm sitting where I can see 50 east. Are you still following the car?"

"Yes, we're getting close to the county line, though."

"Then you aren't far from me. I can take over from here."

"I think I have a better idea," said Charlotte. "Why don't you let us pass and call ahead to the Ocean City police. You can follow us wherever he's going then. Something tells me Ocean City is where he's headed. Let me follow him to the end and then I'll let you know where he is. This isn't a single car theft. I would think we want to nab more than just this one driver. I'd like to get Brenda's Jag back, and this may be our chance."

"OK, it makes sense. But if you hadn't been an FBI agent, you know we couldn't involve a civilian like this. There. I see him coming.

And I can see you a couple of car lengths behind. I've got to duck so he doesn't see anyone in the car. Ringing off now to call the Ocean City police. Call me at the first sign of trouble."

"I will."

Deputy Burch called Charlotte back within fifteen minutes. "OK, the Ocean City police are set up for you to contact through me if that's where the car is going. We'll adjust, if not. But I'm out of my jurisdiction now, so it will need to be the local police wherever we go. Keep this connection open and keep talking to me about where you are and what the Caddie is doing."

Burch rolled up beside Charlotte's Escape where she had stopped outside the entrance of a light industrial park in the western outskirts of Ocean City. Both he and Charlotte got out of their respective cars and he joined her at the front fender of the Escape while other police cars silently glided up. Charlotte talked to the lead cop from the local jurisdiction, who braced up noticeably when Burch took him aside and told him who Charlotte was and who she had been in the FBI.

Then, after Charlotte pointed out which warehouse the Cadillac had pulled into, the cops went ahead on the raid, leaving Charlotte and Dave standing by her car. Burch was called next to go on in. He returned a little later, looking a little shaken.

"You'll have no idea who it was driving the Cadillac," he said as he approached Charlotte.

"My guess is that it was Jason Williams," she said, identifying the owner of Williams' Garage on Penn Street in Hopewell.

"Yes, that's right," he answered, looking quizzically at Charlotte. He started to speak, but Charlotte broke in.

"I hope the other cars were in there. Both Brenda's and Don Dunkel's."

"Yes, they were, just waiting for a load to be shipped down to Rio. There are more than a dozen of them. All specialty cars in some way. They were still in good shape."

"Good. Both Brenda and Don treasure their cars. I don't think new ones would mean nearly the same to either one of them."

"I want to know how you knew it was Jason Williams. All of the signs pointed to his new employee, Billy Zirkel."

"Too many signs pointed to Zirkel for starters," Charlotte said. "I've never known Jason to be so civic minded that he would hire someone on a prison work release. I wondered about that right off the bat. And then Billy said he'd only been picked up by Jason through the state program three weeks ago."

"That's right. So?"

"And when I finally got to talk to Haws Wainwright, he said that Jason was interested in someone who had been in prison for car theft."

"Ah, I'm beginning to see," Dave said.

"The illegal casino resort plan fell through before that. Everyone on the town council was told about it before Brenda and I went down to Florida. Jason is on the town council. He knew chances were good he couldn't complete his expansion and therefore didn't need more help at the garage well before he contacted the state program and hired Billy. I kept my mind open on that—that Jason was hiring and developing a patsy for the car thefts."

"Yes, that makes sense."

"And then I went in to Easton and checked at Jason's bank—after I found out in a conversation which one he used. Jason didn't go to the bank to try to refinance his garage; he went there to deposit a very large sum of money. It wasn't the sort of money one would be making in a short amount of time at Williams' Garage. It was the sort of money one would be paid for stealing expensive cars for an organized car theft ring. Jason was covering his developing losses by stealing rather than more borrowing."

"Does Sheriff Wainwright know what you were figuring out?"

"No, not yet."

"And you didn't tell him your suspicions of Williams because . . . ?"

"I needed more proof. Jason Williams caught driving a stolen car is more proof. And because I've been a little busy with other things since we got back. But I certainly would have said something if Billy Zirkel had been arrested. He's the one I feel sorry for."

"Me too," Dave Burch said. "None of it is his fault, apparently, and now he'll lose his work release program."

"Does it really have to come to that? We'll still need the garage open in Hopewell at least until Jason can be sorted out. Couldn't he just continue there? Perhaps with Don Dunkel supervising him? The church rectory is very close to the garage, and Don pampers that Buick of his so much that he and Billy could be together frequently."

"It's a good idea," Burch said. "I'll talk to Sheriff Wainwright about it."

"If Haws says yes, I'll talk to Don. If that won't work and there's any chance of something else, let Brenda and me know," Charlotte said. "We'd try to set something up that will work."

"That's generous of you. Thanks."

"We need a gas station open in Hopewell," Charlotte answered. "And Billy Zirkel is, as far as I can see, a good fit with a garage. I think he deserves another chance—especially because of what Jason tried to pin on him."

Charlotte went home to Hopewell then, taking with her a promise that Brenda's Jag would be back to her within twenty-four hours, which, of course, delighted Brenda.

"I may keep the Prius for high-mileage trips and to make myself feel 'with it' environmentally," Brenda said. "But I'll drive my baby when I am out just to have the pleasure of driving. We're also keeping the garage locked from now on. What a sad commentary on American life that we have to do that in a small village like Hopewell."

After walking Sam and Rocket and eating a muffin at Zenna's that she decided Brenda and Bea need never know about, Charlotte settled down in the den to start going over Ida Smith's file. She didn't make it even as far as the second page when it hit her what had been bothering her.

"I'm taking the dogs for a walk," she called out from the front door.

"You just got back from walking them," Brenda chimed out from the parlor where she was pouring over the sketches for the retirement home once again. ". . . and from eating a muffin, I might add. It was all over the front of your blouse. Zenna serves great muffins, doesn't she?"

"Yeah, she does," Charlotte answered, full of guilt at having been caught eating, if not at having eaten, the muffin. "But the dogs want to go again."

And they most certainly did want to go again. They hadn't actually been thinking about it, content to lay at Charlotte's feet in the den, which was, by far their second favorite room, the kitchen being their favorite. But all Charlotte had to say was "leash" and suddenly Sam and Rocket didn't want to do anything so much as to take another walk.

It was all subterfuge. If Charlotte walked the streets of the village on her own, suddenly she was inundated with questions from residents on village issues. If she was walking the dogs, most residents gave her a wide berth—not because the dogs were threatening, but because they were too friendly and were champions at supporting the laundry detergent and dry cleaners businesses.

"I wanted to see how you were after that close call with your car," Charlotte said as she entered Hannah Helgerson's house.

"I almost had a heart attack when that sheriff's deputy telephoned me," Hannah answered, as the two women carefully settled in arm chairs that weren't steady on the floor. "If I'd lost that there automobile, my daddy would skin me alive."

Charlotte let the image of a man who had been dead for over three decades skinning the quite hefty and strong-as-an-ox Hannah alive, but she said nothing. She had come for another purpose. And Hannah set Charlotte up for that discussion quite nice and quickly.

"This has become a regular crime center since even before you ran those mobsters out of town," Hannah said. "What with that ghost digging around in the Thompson's yard and now someone stealing honest folks' precious cars. I near croaked when Don Dunkel's nice Buick got took and then my daddy's Cadillac too. I wouldn't wish that on Don Dunkel even though he ain't a Baptist. He's a nice man for a Piscopalian."

"I think the town will quiet down now," Charlotte said. She'd save telling Hannah any more about the arrest of a long-standing village resident. She'd let the grapevine work that one out. And she'd save the news of the retirement community plans for later too. She'd come for a purpose.

"Speaking of the Thompson house, though, I was wondering if you could remember anything about that family."

"Sure can. They were a peculiar bunch—and a little flighty too, and I wouldn't let my sights off them around anything of value for nothing. I turned out to be right about that Muriel Thompson."

"Do you remember if they had any kids?"

"Yep. Two of the them. Little hell-raisers both. A boy and a girl. The girl was worse than the boy."

"Do you remember their names?"

"Of course. That's what makes it so easy to remember them. Horrible names their parents gave them, I'll say. Clarence, the younger, was the boy and Ida was the girl."

There, she'd said it. That was what had lodged in the back of Charlotte's mind from that FBI profile file, the name she'd once known and had forgotten. Ida Thompson. Maybe at some point Ida Thompson, a name given in Ida Smith's file as one of her aliases, had been the woman's real name. It made sense that Ida would eventually take the name of Smith, which was her mother's maiden name.

Hannah had continued to talk, though. ". . . and I always thought it was an act of revenge by them parents."

"Uh, excuse me?" Charlotte said, trying to force her attention back into Hannah's monologue, although Hannah seemed content to be having the conversation all by herself. "What revenge?"

"Why for what their own parents had named them. Muriel. Who names their child Muriel, even in the thirties? And, worse of all, the father's name. Felix."

Bingo, Charlotte thought. Another name from the file. The one given as Ida Smith's father. Felix Thompson. What chances were there that more than one combination of Felix and Ida could crop up in a family with the Thompson surname?

So, this at least explained why Ida Smith had come to Hopewell. She had returned to her childhood home. She'd probably even convinced Edith to come before her just to be here for Ida to use and hide behind. Edith wasn't the brightest bulb in the chandelier.

And, Charlotte went on to think, with a shudder, it just also may lend credence to the possibility that Ida was still floating around the area. Maybe she knew more than anyone else about the legend of the missing bank money. Maybe she had witnessed the aftermath of it as reality.

Charlotte shivered. Maybe the village wasn't safe again at all.

Chapter Five: The Dedication; Twelve Months Later

Even though the construction, furnishing, and staffing of the Curtain Call retirement community facility took a couple of months longer than anyone anticipated, the dedication ceremony for it started off splendidly. And for many it at least seemed to end that way. Not for Charlotte, however. Charlotte thought of this really as Brenda's victory day, so she stayed in the background as much as possible. And it was a good thing she didn't take on any necessary duties, because her day started falling apart even as guests were assembling in the forecourt of the main building.

The day was gorgeous. Late May and not a cloud in sight. The facilities were gorgeous too. Much of Win Engleton's privacy-motivated landscaping on the point property had been preserved, with dense foliage from the front of the main building toward the entrance gate at the end of River Road. But the lawned landscape was mostly cleared from the cottage-façade sides of the three wings to the waters of the Choptank River to the west, south, and east, the property being on a peninsula jutting into the river. The glass corridors of two of the wings faced out to the front of the facility—and those gathering for the dedication and being beckoned to seats on the asphalt of the forecourt—but landscaping had made this view very attractive as well. When the facility was expanded to include cottage façades on the land side, there no doubt would be in fighting on who got what unit among those wanting water views, but, for now the fifteen initial former movie people already in residence had no trouble fitting into the twenty-one existing water-facing units. A few were couples, and the last units on the end of the wings were larger than the others, with an added bedroom, so thus far even the couples were well accommodated.

While the audience facing the slightly raised platform on which Charlotte, mortified at the prospect but a partner of record on the venture, was to stand and say a few words in turn with Brenda and several others, were being shepherded to their seats, Evonne Clagett, the community's executive director, was bustling around making thrice sure that everything was in order. And everything was in order for the dedication ceremony. It was what else started happening that tied Charlotte in knots—and it was mostly happening to her.

Evonne Clagett had been a godsend. She knew what she was doing in putting together a retirement home facility and she was a real dynamo. They would be officially opening much later than this, and would not already be functioning at two-thirds capacity if it hadn't been for Evonne's drive, patience, and skill. She knew how to work with people and she wasn't afraid of rolling up her sleeves and doing whatever work needed to be done even if no one else had stepped up to do it. After Brenda and Charlotte had seen what she could do, they'd left all of the staff hiring to her. Brenda and Charlotte had been so busy with other matters that there were staff members neither had met yet.

Charlotte would normally be clinging to Brenda in a crowd like this, but Brenda had her hands full with other people and with acknowledging the presence of a crowd of people who wanted to be standing in her light in today's victory ceremonies. Strangely enough the new residents of the community weren't after her, although one of them was ever by her side. David Runion, Brenda's long-time leading man and unignited flame was almost glued to her side, in his wheelchair. And, although he didn't seem to be fully aware of where he was, he knew he was on stage and he knew exactly how to act as the leading man on stage. It was just his occasional blank stares and dying off in the middle of speech that confirmed to Charlotte that he wasn't wholly there. He seemed to be fading fast, and Charlotte feared that he wouldn't be with them long and that Brenda had gotten the facility finished and staffed just in time for him.

Even the dogs, Sam and Rocket, seemed to understand how delicate Runion's condition was—and how much Brenda treasured him. They had taken up stations on either side of his wheelchair and were ensuring that no one backed into or stumbled over him.

Besides Runion, and the architect, Douglas Dolan, who could not be denied his limelight on this day, Brenda had her hands full with others who had flown in for the occasion. These included the movie producer, Aaron Woolridge, and the director, Howard Holton, who had been the producing end of an ensemble, including Brenda and David, that had churned out popular film after popular film for three decades. Both not only were speaking at the dedication to add clout to the project, but the two had also voluntarily come through with personal contributions and had cajoled money out of other Hollywood luminaries that had doubled the funds that Brenda had for the project and provided it solid financial backing. And then there was Tony Trice, the young heartthrob role taker in the late years of the ensemble filming. He wasn't there because he had been part of the movie team, though. He was there because he was Brenda's lovechild, which had been kept a secret from him until the last couple of years. Brenda had given birth to him before she had become a star. When she had gone to Hollywood, she had left him behind but always kept track of him, and when she had become a star, she made sure there was a place in the movies for him too. He came by his acting talent—and startling good looks—honestly, though, through Brenda.

Tony wasn't speaking today, but he certainly was a center of attention—not so much from the initial residents of the retirement community, who, as movie folks themselves, had seen all the greats come and go already, but more from the local village residents who had been invited and the inevitable media folks who couldn't be kept away. His presence was enhanced by the new girlfriend he'd brought with him, a ragingly popular professional tennis star of the present—the eminently photogenic, Michelle Minor.

The first hedge on Charlotte enjoying the day was just a curious nagging in the back of her mind. A refreshment table was serving off to the side and she caught sight of someone from the back standing there who reminded her immediately of someone she never wanted to see again. But it was only after she'd scanned away from the table and then back to find that the figure had left that it occurred to her that something was entirely too familiar with that stance. She was about to worry more about what she had seen—something that she painfully was aware would have come to her in a flash in her career days—when, speaking of her career days, Evan Worthington walked up to her.

"Evan!" she exclaimed, showing more surprise and confusion than pleasure apparently, as Evan—who was still sharp as a tack and still working his FBI career—was quick to pick up on the atmospherics.

"Good to see you too, Charlotte. Did I interrupt something? You seem to be miles away."

"Umm, I just saw someone I thought I knew from long ago, but it couldn't be. I'm just surprised that you're here."

"I did receive an invitation, you know."

"No, I didn't know." She immediately regretted saying that, as, though it did reflect her not fully successful attempts to keep him at arm's length over the past year, she didn't really want it to sound that way. Of course he would have been invited. Brenda continued to be close friends with Douglas Dolan throughout the planning and construction phase of the retirement community building, if not quite the type of friend Douglas obviously wanted her to be. And Douglas and Evan got along famously. So, for the past nearly a year, at Brenda's initiation, there had been many "double dates" involving the four, quite a few of them on Douglas' yacht. So, of course he would have been invited to the dedication. It just wasn't Charlotte who planned the invitations.

She added, "I mean I didn't know you'd received an invitation, as Brenda didn't let me get anywhere close to the invitation list. If she had, this dedication would have been just Brenda and me, drinking coffee, over the breakfast table. If you can remember such things, I have an aversion to celebrations like this. But of course you would have been invited. It's just that it's an awful long way to come, from Annapolis to here on a weekday just to listen to a few repetitive speeches and watch a few back pats."

"Yes, I most certainly do remember your reclusiveness. I would have come just to watch you try to fade into the foliage during this. When you have every right to be front and center. I know how much work you've put into this. But the lieutenant governor came from Annapolis to cut the ribbon, so why shouldn't I? Besides, I came in an official capacity. And it's something I need to talk to you about, before—"

But then Evonne Clagett was on the rostrum, banging a Chinese gong she had found somewhere and telling them all to find their seats because the dedication ceremony was about to begin. Evan gave Charlotte a concerned look, but then smiled and told her to go on to her seat of honor on the front row facing the platform—that they'd talk later.

Charlotte's day just kept on crumbling, though, as she inserted her bulk into the milling mass of people going to their seats. She was half way up the aisle, when she almost stumbled over an elderly, hunched-over woman with a walker who Charlotte hadn't focused on because she was unusually tall and the woman was unusually not.

"You," the woman muttered. "I'd heard you were in on this with . . . that woman . . . so I guessed you'd be stomping on me with those big feet of yours at some point."

"Gladys?" Charlotte exclaimed, not having a bit of trouble recognizing a woman who had plagued her for far more years than she should have put up with. "What are you doing here?"

"I live here, bitch," was the terse and acidic reply.

Yep, that was Gladys Morrison, Charlotte thought.

But then they were parted in the swirl of people around her and Charlotte was at the front row and sitting down beside Brenda.

"What's the matter, Charlotte?" Brenda asked after taking a look at Charlotte's ashen complexion and "deer in the headlights" expression. "You look like you've seen a ghost, if you'll excuse the cliché."

"I think I have. At least I thought the women had gone on to all of our rewards some time ago."

"Who did you see?"

"My mother-in-law. Well, my former mother-in-law. Gladys Morrison. I wouldn't in a million years have expected to see her here."

"Gladys Morrison? Gladys Morrison is your former mother-in-law?" Brenda laughed, but then when she saw that Charlotte wasn't laughing with her, she stopped. "Gladys is one of the new residents. She was Helga's wardrobe mistress for years."

Helga Lund, once a leading costume designer for the movies, had been the woman Brenda had lived with in Hollywood for some years up until she died, murdered by being hung from a chandelier in the foyer of Brenda's Hollywood Hills house. Brenda had been suspected in the murder and Charlotte had cleared her and solved the murder, which was just after the two woman started becoming close.

"I didn't know that. I got her later in life when she'd turned into a witch."

"She always was a witch," Brenda said. "She was happy to believe I'd killed Helga."

"Yes, she gave me that impression just now. And yet you've included her on your resident's list."

"Yes. She needed someplace to live out her life for free. And she was a worker in the movie industry—at the same studio I worked for."

"You are a saint, Brenda," Charlotte said. She was going on to say something about perhaps being too much of a saint, but Evonne Clagett was beating on her gong for order.

The gathering wasn't quieting down quickly, though, probably because, in Evonne's only mistake of the day, the refreshments table had been opened too soon. Charlotte took those few moments to recall the familiar figure she'd seen at the refreshment table, to link it to the appearance of Gladys Morrison, and to turn and scan the crowd.

Delores Morrison's purple fingernail polish gave them away. If it hadn't been for that, Charlotte's gaze would have continued on over the visage of her former husband, Sydney Morrison, and his new wife, and former secretary, Delores. They both had changed—or been changed—significantly. Sydney had put on weight, had grown a beard, and was almost fully gray now. Delores had gone the "try-to-look-younger" route, with an obvious face lift—she looked like she had no other possible expression available to her than a pinched smile—and a dark auburn hairdo, with impossibly scarlet highlights. Delores had once been a proud bottle blonde.

It made sense now. They were here to make sure that Sydney's mother, Gladys, had been put away for good. Sydney couldn't stomach his mother any better than Charlotte ever had.

The surprise of seeing them here—or anywhere—though, was because the last Charlotte knew they were on the lam from some very serious-minded mobsters who thought that Sydney and his new beloved, who had been Sydney's secretary when he was married to Charlotte, had screwed them royally, much more royally than Sydney had ever screwed Charlotte. After parting ways with Charlotte and marrying Delores, who, under the maiden name of Crea, was from a leading New Jersey mob family, Sydney had run an Ocean City casino, fronting for the Crea family, and, with Delores's help, had proceeded to noticeably embezzle the casino profits, not leaving nearly enough for the Crea family to embezzle itself. Thus, a contract had been put out on the Morrisons, who had tried to embroil both Charlotte and Brenda in their troubles, and they had scooted out of town and out of sight, if not out of mind.

The last Charlotte had seen of the pair was them cowering in her cottage, having gotten embroiled in the aborted illegal casino resort deal that had preceded the conversion of this property into a retirement community. With the full forces of the New Jersey mob families on their tail, Charlotte hadn't figured on seeing Sydney and his most recent bride ever again—certainly not alive.

Charlotte didn't wish them dead, but she also didn't particularly wish them well—and she certainly wished them to be anywhere but here.

They had seen her now, looking back into the seated crowd from the front row, and both automatically dipped their heads. They didn't do so, though, before Charlotte gave them both the evil eye. She'd already done them the last favor she ever would—particularly because they had involved Brenda in their problems and even had kidnapped her briefly. Charlotte hadn't turned them in when she found them hiding from everyone else in her cottage.

With the exception of the occasional sound of the grating of metal on metal where, the construction on the central building having been completed, the construction crew had now turned to clearing the collapsed houses out farther on River Street, the rest of the ceremony went off nearly as flawlessly as Evonne Clagett had carefully planned. The single exception was that when Brenda returned to her chair after giving her customarily charming speech, she apparently showed that underneath it all she had as much a case of the nerves as anyone else, because she missed her chair when she sat down, almost turning David Runion's wheelchair over in the process as she grabbed for its arm when she unsuccessfully tried to maintain her balance. Charlotte had to scoop her off the ground.

Charlotte heard an ominous groan from Brenda. "You OK?" she whispered as she lifted the woman up.

"I think I sprained my ankle. I may need support later when we're all standing."

"You'll have it," Charlotte declared.

And then they were all at the front door of the building and the lieutenant governor, Brenda, Charlotte, Aaron Woolridge, Howard Holton, Evonne Clagett, and, representing the residents, David Runion, were all there cutting the ribbon that symbolized the facility was formally up and running.

Tony Trice had seen Charlotte help Brenda up to the ribbon cutting, and immediately thereafter, he was at their elbow, saying, "Here, let me do that, Charlotte."

Charlotte wasn't about to mess with the love between a son and his mother, an affection that had gone unexercised for so long, and she backed off gracefully with a smile for Tony. Even after having found out that Brenda was his mother, Tony hadn't batted an eye over her relationship with Charlotte, and Charlotte was eternally grateful to him for that.

When Charlotte backed away from Brenda and Tony, who were swamped again by well-wishers and those wanting to press the flesh with movie stars, she backed right into the arms of Evan Worthington. She turned and grimaced at him.

"You've seen them, I take it," Evan said.

"Seen who?"

"The Morrisons. I wanted to warn you that they're here, but I saw you turn right before the ceremony started and see them sitting back there. They are the reason why I'm here. I told you I had an official reason to be here."

"You somehow surmised they'd be here to see Sydney's mother put into the home and you're here to arrest them?" Charlotte had a sudden favorable impression of Evan being here.

"Not exactly. They are in the witness protection program. Have been for over a year. I couldn't tell you that. But Sydney said he wanted to see his mother one last time. Not that she knows he's here and I got the impression he wants to see that she's pinned down rather than that she's being taken care of. But he said he'd be here one way or the other. So I brought him here and I'll take him away. And you'll never be bothered by him again. He and Delores—mostly Delores, I must say—have given valuable information on the workings of the New Jersey mob. It was well worth not prosecuting the two. I hope you can understand that—especially because you and Brenda have more reason than most to want them prosecuted for wrongs done both of you."

"No, vengeance against those two doesn't interest me. Sydney's too much of a worm to hold a grudge against, and Delores' just punishment is in winding up with Sydney. If you just promise I'm well rid of them, that's enough for me. Brenda, being Brenda and only looking for the good in people, has, I'm sure already forgotten all about them."

"I promise then. So, it's been a good day for Brenda?"

"I hope so," Charlotte answered. "But part of this trait of hers in only seeing the good in people may have become a problem for her here."

"Oh? How so."

"Because of what I see in Sydney's mother, Gladys, and in a couple of the other residents who have been given a free ride here. Look out over the crowd. Who stands out and why?"

"You mean other than Sydney and Delores, looking at us nervously."

"Yes," Charlotte said, with a laugh. "Other than those two, who I refuse to acknowledge are even here. Look over to that group of residents gathered around Sydney's mother."

"They look grumpy. Being curmudgeons at that age, though, is to be expected of many people."

"Yes, but I've seen some of them giving Brenda far from friendly looks. And in the moment I talked with Gladys, it's clear to me that she doesn't see Brenda as the savior you and I know she is. She talked of Brenda with resentment, something close to the hatred she openly expressed for me. And Brenda told me that Gladys has continued to say Brenda killed Helga Lund, even when she knows otherwise. I'm afraid it's not going to be all paradise for Brenda with these folks she's helping. I just hope she won't be hurt by the lack of gratitude of some of them."

"I hope so too," Evan said. "We'll just have to fill in the cracks on any feelings of gratitude toward her—you and I—then."

Charlotte could easily have kissed Evan then, and she came close to doing so. But, probably because of bad timing on his part as he'd been playing for that kiss for over a year, he had turned his face from hers to see where the Morrisons were huddling.

"I guess it's time for me to get those two back under wraps," he said.

"Yes, I guess so. I take it that they aren't living as far away as I would hope they were."

"You know I can't answer that, Charlotte. All I can say is that they are bored stiff at being held so closely under guard. And that it won't be a piece of cake for them when we start producing them for a series of trials that they've provided evidence for."

"Good," Charlotte said.

Then Evan did act like he wanted a kiss as he was turning away to escort the Morrisons off the grounds, but the moment had passed for Charlotte and he had to do with an affectionate hug.

As she watched Evan walk across the forecourt and gather up Sydney and Delores, she let her gaze travel over the crowd again. Other than the sourpusses standing and leaning on their walkers around Gladys Morrison, it looked like everyone else was still euphoric. She didn't, however, sweep far enough around the gathering. There at the edge of the crowd, dressed in a nurse's uniform, stood a figure who wasn't smiling, that, in fact, was looking very grim and doing a separate assessment of the mood and interaction of the players on the scene with a shrewd and highly calculating inventory.

A voice behind her brought Charlotte back to the gathering.

"He's a good man."

Charlotte knew the voice. Don Dunkel, the Episcopalian minister, but as she watched both Evan and Sydney walk away, she didn't completely latch into who he was talking about.

"Hello, Don. I hope you're enjoying yourself. Who's a good man?"

"That FBI agent, Evan Worthington. He's a good man."

"Yes he is." She felt a bit trapped. She felt that Don genuinely liked Brenda and her and was resigned to tolerate their relationship, but Charlotte didn't think that Don was a progressive Episcopalian even though his heart was in the right place. She was fairly certain he was concerned about her relationship with Brenda and couldn't shake the belief they were living in sin. She changed the subject as quickly as she could.

"And you are a good man, too, Don. You've done wonders with Bill Zirkel at the garage."

"He has turned out to be an excellent worker and businessman. But he wouldn't even be here, and I wouldn't be in the position to guide him, if you and Brenda hadn't bought the garage from Jason and worked out a work-to-purchase plan with Bill."

"The village can't do without a gas station and routine and emergency repairs garage, and the poor guy was getting a raw deal in being set up by Jason to take the fall for the car thefts. How goes it at the church? More folks coming back since you got the new, expanded front put on it?"

"A few from the retirement community here already, yes, both residents and staff," Don answered, although he looked a little worried. "Quite a few are going across the street to the Baptists, though. Hannah Helgerson is good at pestering people and the church building is brand new. And I've heard that people like the livelier music they have over there. Who knew that Mary Miller could play the organ like that?"

"Mary is a woman of many talents. And she and Walt have been downright jolly since their beauty salon and barbershop businesses have stepped up."

"You and Brenda aren't thinking of absconding to the Baptists, are you? Having Hannah's niece under your roof and all, I thought that you might be—"

"Not a chance, Don. I can't carry a tune and Brenda loves the pageantry of your service; the Baptists are too simplistic for her. They would throw us both out of their building half way through the first service we attended."

That wasn't the real reason they wouldn't consider switching, though. The Baptist service started an hour before the Episcopal one and lasted a good half an hour longer. Brenda couldn't get up that early or sit through a church service that long and the two of them were only going to any church out of loyalty to Don Dunkel. She could see now, though, as relieved as Don looked, that he had been genuinely worried about losing them.

"You can bank on us, Don. We're staying with you. Bea doesn't go to any church, so I don't think Hannah has any leverage with her in that department. If you need higher attendance numbers to bolster your record with your superiors, we could always bring Sam and Rocket to church. Whenever I pass the Baptist church when they're singing, the singing sets both of them to howling, so I'm sure they'd prefer your service."

Dunkel laughed, and Charlotte saw the color come back into his face. "I don't think it will come to that—but I'll certainly keep it in mind. And, if you don't feel I'm deserting you, I have a few more pleas to make as long as we seem to have the whole village here."

113

"Go forth and onward Christian soldiers against those Baptists," Charlotte said, with a laugh. Don walked off and Charlotte scanned the crowd again, with her gaze eventually turning toward the front gate out into River Street, where Deputy Sheriff Dave Burch now was standing. He obviously was looking for someone, and that someone obviously was Charlotte. He motioned her over and Charlotte moved casually in his direction, sensing that there was a problem that no one else need know about at this moment.

She was right.

"Hello, Dave. Are you late or weren't you invited? And before you answer that, I will let you know that I wasn't allowed to work on the invitations."

"I'm on the job, Ms. Diamond. And I'm afraid it's pretty grim. When you can come away from here without it being noticed, could you come to the property that was across from your cottage? I don't want anyone from here but you to know for now, but I thought I should clue you in."

"I can say the dogs need to be walked. Sam and Rocket can always be convincing that they need a walk if they see there's a possibility of it. Go ahead over and I'll be there in a few minutes."

When she and the dogs had approached the house, she could see that the bulldozing had stopped but that most of the debris from the collapsed house she now thought of as the Thompson house had been bulldozed away and was in the back of three dump trucks. The workers were standing around their vehicles and smoking and talking among themselves. Dave Burch and another deputy sheriff were standing next to the hole that was left when the Thompson house debris had been cleared.

"Apparently no one knew there was a half cellar under this house," Burch said as Charlotte was pulled up beside him by suddenly very interested dogs.

"No, I didn't know either," Charlotte answered, as she looked down into the cellar hole.

"Can you see it down there?"

"Yes. It's a skeleton wrapped in deteriorating burlap, I take it?"

"Yes. We've got a call out for the medical examiner. Don't know anything more now but that it's a skeleton. But I can tell you what else we found down there—what the skeleton was hugging."

"What?"

"A lot of old, moldy banknotes. Stacks of them."

"Ah, the legend lives," Charlotte said. But she wasn't surprised. Her premonition that Ida Thompson Smith was still around here for some reason or another had now found its cause.

Chapter Six: Grumpy Foursome

Charlotte had convinced Dave Burch to tamp down the police presence at the Thompson house site until after all of the celebrants at the retirement home dedication had cleared the area. She had established the identification of this as the Thompson house in her mind, and she'd spent considerable time trying to find out all she could about that family after learning that it was almost definite that Ida Smith was the daughter of the people who had lived here at one time and whose residency had been linked to an unsolved bank robbery. That she couldn't find any evidence of what had happened to anyone in the family other than the mother, Muriel, who was tracked down, convicted for the bank robbery, served time, and then disappeared—only convinced Charlotte more that there had been more going on with that family than had come to light since. There had been no trace of what had happened to the two children.

Burch hadn't been too keen on calling the medical examiner and sheriff to hold off coming before the dedication crowd cleared until Charlotte had pointed out that the media was inside the retirement home compound and undoubtedly would just love to run off in speculation about what had happened here. Then Burch couldn't punch the buttons on his cell phone fast enough.

Charlotte went back to the compound to whisper to Brenda what was happening outside and do her duty in the farewelling (and unspoken "just get going") of the guests. She left Brenda in Tony's supportive hands and went back to talk with Dave Burch at the Thompson house site after she'd made sure the last of the media had cleared. This wasn't before she'd waved the architect, Douglas Dolan, and the lieutenant governor and his minders off on Douglas' yacht. The movie director Howard Holton and producer Aaron Woodridge were with them, as well, having been invited to the state house in Annapolis for a formal dinner with the governor, who wanted to promote Maryland as a movie set location. The one thing the mobsters had gotten constructed before their casino scheme collapsed about them was a first-rate pier for large boats. This is how they had planned to ship in their privacy-seeking casino guests to and from the resort. Now it served as the perfect means for official state guests to get here from Annapolis and back again.

"I'll bet you have some idea who we've found down here," Burch said when Charlotte returned to his side. "You didn't tell me why you weren't surprised at what we found before you got me started on delaying discovery here."

"Are you sorry I suggested you hold everyone off?"

"Not in the slightest. Sheriff Wainwright saw immediately the need to let the media clear from your event first—and he specifically noted needing to let the lieutenant governor get off site. He thought I was being brilliant in suggesting he and the medical examiner hold off. I hope you don't mind that I let him think that. I need the credit with him."

"No, I don't mind, although I don't think it's flattery to say I think it's usually the sheriff who needs to come up to your mark. We couldn't be more delighted here in Hopewell that you're the deputy protecting us."

"Thanks, Ms. Diamond. That means a lot coming from you. But, back to this skeleton and the money. Can you wager a guess who that is down there? You already told me the village legend that there may be bank heist money buried around here."

"If it's a man, I'd guess it's Felix Thompson and if it's a woman, I think it's probably his wife, Muriel. She went to prison for the bank heist and he just disappeared. And after prison she disappeared too. My money would be on it being Felix and that he didn't live to move away from here at all—perhaps by Muriel's decision. If it was Muriel, she came back after prison to recover the money and someone was waiting for her here. If that's what happened, this is still a wide-open case. Muriel was the only one apprehended in the bank robbery. It's unlikely she was the only one involved in that, though."

"And why have you delved so deeply into this?"

"I didn't tell you the whole story—didn't even know then what I know now about it—back when I was suggesting that Ida Smith may still be lurking around in the area nearly a year ago and even that she may have been the one other than Joyce Vale digging around on this property. My research indicates that Ida Smith was originally Ida Thompson and lived here as the daughter of Felix and Muriel at the time of the bank heist and what came afterward. I think she's been floating around here trying to recover that money. She was just too young at the time to know where, exactly, it had been buried. She may not even have known about this small cellar under the house. A question, though, is what, if anything, she knows about the skeleton down there."

"Guess we'll get a few more answers now," Burch said. "I see that here come the medical examiner and an ambulance. And Sheriff Wainwright is in their wake. A question. I think Sheriff Wainwright will want to know why this excavation was going on. Do you know why?"

"Yes, of course. This is part of the retirement community land, as is what's across the street, including to the northern boundary of where my cottage still stands. We didn't have the money to build the whole planned complex at once, so only the main building is now up. But more money is coming in, so construction has started up again. This is going to be a guest complex—for family coming to visit the residents—and a community center, with pool, and some amenity shops and a small library—so the residents can get a little bit of a walk, but don't have to go all of the way into town, if they don't want to. But it won't take business from the villagers. Those with businesses there will have hours open here too, including a small beauty salon and barbershop run by the Millers. Across the street will be a second residential facility, probably more assisted living and rehab center and more extensive medical facilities than we now have in the main building. My cottage, which is the construction office now, will be turned into a visitors' and information center."

Charlotte didn't want to say more about that building, which was somewhat of a sticky issue between her and Brenda. Brenda was insisting that the cottage remain standing and that property remain in Charlotte's name so that Charlotte would always have someplace to retreat to. Charlotte said that it was a question mark on the strength of their relationship, but Brenda insisted that it was insurance that would keep the strain off their relationship.

Burch didn't have an opportunity to ask any follow-up questions, because the police entourage had arrived and car doors were opening.

"I'll give my hellos and retreat back to the retirement center," Charlotte said quietly to Burch. "I really do have duties back there."

Beyond needing to get back to Brenda and their guests, though, she didn't want to stand in Dave's light on this find, and both Sheriff Wainwright and the medical examiner wouldn't be all that pleased to see Charlotte's fingers in another county criminal investigation. The medical examiner, Sharon Como, was someone Charlotte had known since her days at the FBI training academy in Quantico, Virginia, and who— somewhat uncomfortably for both of them, although Charlotte liked Sharon—had known both Charlotte and Evan in the period during which the two had been dating hot and heavy. Even more uncomfortably, Sharon had shown a similar interest in Charlotte as Evan had at the time. Although that hadn't gone anywhere, it was the very first inkling that Charlotte could have a sexual interest in another woman.

"Hello, Sharon . . . Sheriff," Charlotte said as the two walked up to her, the expressions on Wainwright's face not being the happiest at seeing her here. "I was just getting back to the retirement community building. I was helping Deputy Burch make sure that the festivities there didn't intrude on your crime scene."

She was already moving away from them, and neither the medical examiner nor the sheriff made any effort to keep her there. She trusted that Dave Burch would be able to fill them in on everything that needed to be known while dragging what Charlotte knew and suspected—as being what Charlotte knew and suspected—in to the report as little as possible. Charlotte also knew that Dave would call her later this evening and fill her in on anything and everything subsequently discovered or decided.

* * * *

"Brenda! What's happened to you? You weren't banged up like this just from missing the chair."

Charlotte had entered the dining room of the retirement center, which was also functioning as the games room when meals weren't being served. Brenda and Tony were sitting in chairs around a circular table, David Runion was pushed up to the table in his wheelchair, and Evonne Clagett was kneeling on the floor next to Brenda and washing off a bloodied area on her calf. And it wasn't the calf of the leg with the ankle Brenda had sprained earlier. Brenda was sitting sideways to the table and had both of her legs up in a chair. As she worked on the leg, Evonne told them that she thought Brenda had sprained the other ankle as well.

Through the two-story plate-glass window looking out over the rear lawn and a sweep of the Choptank River, Charlotte could see Tony's girlfriend, Michelle Minor, talking with a couple of the residents on the back patio. She had a tennis racket and was showing them something about her racket stroke. Tony had been linked with several women over the past several years, some starlets and a few in sports, and, by far, Charlotte preferred the sportswomen—and Michelle was the least conceited and self-centered of them all.

"She lost her balance and fell down the front steps as we were coming back into the building," Tony offered.

"I felt like I was pulled off balance," Brenda said weakly.

"Let's get you on home," Charlotte said. "This is two accidents too many."

Evonne saw movement out of the corner of her eye. The physical therapist she'd called on her cell phone to bring salve and a bandage into the dayroom was in the doorway from one of the wings, but the woman turned abruptly around and left again. Giving a little scowl, Evonne stood up.

"I'll be back in a minute with something to put on that. I guess we should postpone the review session we were going to have for now."

"No, please," Brenda said. "It's a good day to do this, so let's do it."

She was looking at David Runion, and all understood what she meant. Since the crowd had dispersed, Runion had been as coherent as he ever was these days. Relieved of the need to perform, Runion had relaxed. Days like this were fewer and fewer, and Brenda saw the need to take the greatest advantage of them. Brenda's perceived need for David in this meeting was that he now was heavily invested in the retirement community. Most of the residents were destitute and were here on full sufferance. Runion and a few others weren't. Once he had warmed to the idea of coming here, he had insisted on paying his own way and more. And beyond that, he had rewritten his will so that the community would get the lion's share of his extensive estate after he died. No one was saying anything, but all had been thinking that David's death wasn't too far off now. Brenda wanted to be quite sure that this support for the retirement community was what he wanted his legacy to be.

Tony didn't have to be there, but he was solicitous of Brenda having fallen twice today, once while he was supporting her, and he would be glued to her until she got home and safely in her own bed.

While they were waiting for Evonne to return, Charlotte looked out over the dining room. Besides those around this table, there were only five other people in the room. Four of them were residents, two women and two men, all sitting around a table playing cards—and rather viciously so, slapping their cards down hard on the table, giving sour looks, and muttering to each other in sotto voce. One of the men was in a wheelchair. Sitting off from them, but obviously on duty in case she was needed, was a middle-aged woman in a uniform that probably was a nurse's uniform but that was cut and in a color that wouldn't immediately identify it as being institutional.

Charlotte could see that the four residents weren't keeping their sour looks to each other, but that each occasionally looked over at the table where Charlotte and the others were sitting and casting their scowls generously in that direction. One of the women was Charlotte's former mother-in-law, Gladys Morrison. Charlotte couldn't help but think, with a touch of amusement, that Gladys had found a group here she fit right in with, so she must have found ninth heaven even without the requirement of actually dying.

After their meeting was over, David Runion, who had managed to remain lucid the entire time surprised them by asking Charlotte to wheel him back to his unit. It was Brenda who he had clung to today— and had done so since he'd moved into the facility—but Charlotte silently congratulated him on the evidence that he truly was having a good day. Brenda was out of commission now, and Tony obviously wanted to be the one to drive her back to the house, so Charlotte was the most logical person to help David back to his cottage.

As Charlotte wheeled Runion through the door from the glassed-in corridor into his cottage, he put a hand on her forearm and said, "Can you stay just a moment, Charlotte? I want to ask you to do something for me."

"Yes, of course, David. What's on your mind?"

"Did you see the four at the card table? And how they shot those ugly looks at Brenda?"

"Yes I saw them. But are you sure they were looking at Brenda? You may not know that one of those is my former mother-in-law, and we do not and never did get along. She may just have been telling tales on me that made the others share in her anger."

"Yes. That's Gladys. She makes no secret of her hates. And she hates Brenda more than she hates you. And those other three hate Brenda too."

"Why?"

"Water under the bridge. But I can tell you that none of it was Brenda's fault. She's an angel. Maybe a bit of a sap too, to let those four in here. But what I want you to do for me is to keep a good eye on Brenda and keep those four away from her."

"You think four old people are a physical threat to Brenda?" Charlotte asked, not able to hide the disbelief in her voice. "One of them is even in a wheelchair."

"I'm in a wheelchair. That's why I need someone else close to Brenda wary of them and watching out for her."

"Yes, of course I will, David. But really? Those four are a physical threat to Brenda?"

"You don't think she's had those two accidents today all on her own, do you?"

Charlotte didn't argue from that point, although it sounded like David was being paranoid. It seemed to her that David Runion's good, lucid day was coming to a quick close.

* * * *

Not long after Charlotte had made it home and checked on Brenda in bed; on Sam and Rocket sitting by Brenda, their muzzles on the bed and looking mournfully at their stricken mistress; on Bea humming and preparing dinner in the kitchen; and on Tony and Michelle sitting in the family room, drinking cocktails, comparing notes from the day, and cogitating where the nightlife might be best, northeast to Easton or southeast to Cambridge, Charlotte received the telephone call she'd been waiting for from Deputy Burch.

"Medical examiner says it's the skeleton of a man. Probably there from the fifties."

"That would be right for Felix Thompson, then," Charlotte said.

"Yes, that's what we think too. We can pretty much confirm it. We have Ida Smith's DNA records that the FBI gave us for the Edna Smith murder. If hers is in the same family as this skeleton's, that will be pretty conclusive. And we've traced the bands on the banknotes back to the bank in Cambridge where Muriel Thompson worked and that was robbed. The banknotes have pretty much deteriorated, but the bank says it can recover the value when we are able to release it."

"That's that then."

"Yes, for now. I did tell Sheriff Wainwright that most of the sleuthing came from you. He said to thank you."

"Through gnashing teeth, I'm sure, Dave. You know you didn't have to do that. We're on the same team, you and I, and I'm sure that Wainwright even would have been happier if the information was from you."

"Yes, ma'am, but I thought about it and right is right."

"Let me know if there's anything else to be gleaned from this, Dave, but, truthfully, I hope I won't hear from you on a case for a while."

"Yes, ma'am, I understand."

After she clicked off the call, she went into the den and gave Tony and Michelle the bad news. For international celebrities like them, there wasn't much of a night life choice between Easton and Cambridge. In fact, there wasn't much of an option in either. The two decided to stay in for the night and watch old movies—and Charlotte got the sense that Michelle was relieved by that choice, which just added a notch on Michelle's "good catch" belt, as far as Charlotte was concerned.

She turned in early. Brenda hadn't been able to come down to dinner, and after walking the dogs and deciding that Tony and Michelle really didn't need help—or company—while they cuddled and watched old movies, Charlotte decided to spend the evening where Brenda was, with both of them reading novels until the mood struck them to cuddle as well.

Before they turned out the lights, Charlotte remembered her last conversation with David Runion and decided to ask Brenda about the "grumpy four" without revealing that David had expressed concern.

"Yes, they are a little grumpy, aren't they?" Brenda said. "And it just deepens for them to have found each other and encouraged each other to be miserable. Gladys you know about. I find the coincidence amusing that you two are connected. The other woman is Betty Bentley. She was an actress somewhat older than me whose career never seemed to take off. I'm afraid I never thought she was a very good actress. She probably sensed that was what I felt. The man in the wheelchair is Phil Taylor. He was a movie cameraman, the beau of Helga, I understand, while he was still working for the studio. We worked in several movies together. But he moved on to independent films where he had more personal control. I think he did quite well too. It was the last film I worked on with him, though, that he hurt his legs. He was filming me on a ledge in a jungle scene, and he went over the side. Poor man. The other man is Stan Plaugher. He was what we called a grip in the movies. One of the men who moved sets around. We worked on some of the same movies, but he had trouble with drink. He almost beaned David and me with a heavy backdrop one day by leaning against it. Howard said he'd come to work drunk and fired him. But he'd already been in the movies several years. I think he went to Las Vegas and worked on stages there afterward. I didn't find him; he wasn't on my original list of possible residents. He heard about what we were doing and applied. He was almost homeless, so I was happy to include him."

"They sound like a belligerent bunch," Charlotte said. "And all seem not to be very grateful to you. They worry me. And I'll have to admit that I think they worry David too. They might be unpleasant with you. I wonder why you included them in the community at all."

"To be honest, I've always worried about those four and whether I had been unfair to them and helped cause the resentment they feel."

"Why on earth would you feel responsible for them, Brenda?"

"They all lost something and I was involved in that. Aaron took Betty Bentley off a movie with me because he said she kept stepping on my lines—and not in a good way for either of us. I'm sure she thought I complained, but I didn't. I'm sure Aaron sensed I didn't like it, though. Both Phil and Stan got fired because of something involving me. And I'm afraid I was a little short with Stan when that backdrop fell. If it had hit either David or me, I'm sure we would have been killed. I just lost it there for a moment. And you know that Gladys can't absolve me of Helga's death."

"Well, you're a saint to take them in, that's all I can say," Charlotte said. And before she turned off the light, she added, "Let's just stay well away from them if we can, shall we? Giving them a free ride to the end of their days seems more than generous for any guilt you might feel. Although I think that guilt is probably misguided even if those four grumps wouldn't."

Shortly after dawn the next morning, Charlotte's cell phone softly buzzed, and she picked it up as quickly and quietly as she could. She was a lighter sleeper than Brenda anyway—and rose earlier on any given day—but Brenda's legs had been in pain when they were trying to go to sleep and Charlotte had brought her sleeping pills that still had her dead to the world.

"Yes, this is Charlotte," she whispered into her phone as she carefully got out of bed, almost tripped over two suddenly very interested dogs, and stole into the dressing room between their bedroom and bath. The dogs came right along with her. She had the pocket door closed before the woman on the other line, who was having trouble controlling her voice, could speak.

"Please, you need to come to the home, Charlotte. Right now, if you can." It was Evonne Clagett, and if she ever was able to display panic in her voice, she was doing so now.

"What is it? Is something—?"

"Please hurry. You'll see when you get here. But, please don't say anything to Brenda. She shouldn't know yet." And then Evonne hung up.

Charlotte dressed quickly. The dogs looked at her in expectation. One of their mistresses was up and about. She always was the one up early. They were going to get to go for a walk. This was the routine.

Charlotte whispered to them, "Sorry, guys, not yet today."

They, of course, interpreted that to mean, "Let's go find your leashes."

They were trotting along on either side of her as she walked out into the hall and silently shut the bedroom door behind her. Tony was standing in the hall in his dressing gown.

They had both heard the police car and ambulance sirens as they had just passed the house toward the end of River Street.

"What do you think—?" Tony started to say.

"I got a call. It's something at the retirement center. I'll drive down. Evonne wants me there. And she specifically said she didn't want

130

Brenda there. Brenda's zonked on sleeping pills. And these dogs are going to be pills themselves and will howl if I don't take them for a walk."

"Do you want me to take them? We could go out of the house together and to the garage and then I could take them from there. By then they should just be pleased they're being walked and not care that it isn't you or Brenda walking them. I can get them out of howling distance as quickly as possible."

"Could you, please? Thank you."

Michelle was there now too. And she was dressed, although she was still tucking her top into her jeans. "I'll walk them too. They seem to like me," she said.

"Michelle, you are a gem. Michelle is a keeper, Tony," Charlotte said. And then, as soon as Tony was dressed, which he did quickly, they were off.

Charlotte could see the problem as she walked up the front steps of the retirement center. The double front doors were wide. She almost stopped in her tracks as soon as she realized what had happened, and, if it hadn't been for her FBI training and long, hard career, she might have gone to the side of the stairs to retch.

The body of David Runion was hanging from the massive center chandelier in the entrance foyer of the retirement center building. His wheelchair was on its side below him.

As Charlotte entered the building and joined the group of sheriff deputies, including Dave Burch, and paramedics, still standing there in shock themselves, Gladys Morrison, dressed sloppily in a ratty terrycloth robe and bunny slippers, her hair in curlers, appeared in the

131

doorway to one of the cottage wings. She let out a piercing scream, which ended in a deathly cry.

"She's done it again! The bitch has killed again! This time for money!"

Charlotte and everyone else turned a shocked look toward the doorway where Gladys stood. As quickly as she was there, though, she was gone. A woman wearing one of the staff uniforms made to not look like an institutional uniform, appeared behind Gladys in the doorway, enfolded Gladys in her arms, and pulled her into the dark corridor of the residential wing beyond.

Shock mounting on shock, Charlotte suffered a moment's paralysis, a hesitation that she later would cite to Brenda as further proof that she was losing the edge she'd had when she was an active FBI agent. But then she was on the move, pushing Evonne Clagett, sheriff's deputies, and paramedics aside as she lumbered across the foyer, past the still-swinging body of David Runion, and through the door to the darkened doorway through which Gladys had been dragged by the staff nurse.

She returned moments later, though, looking perplexed, angry, and at least momentarily defeated.

"What was that all about? Who was that woman claiming had killed this guy?" Dave Burch stepped forward to ask.

"Forget her," Charlotte snapped. "She's looneybins. That nurse who pulled her away. That was Ida Smith. That's who we must find."

Chapter Seven: Not What It Seems

"I don't know why you are even bothering with the crazy woman's blathering," Charlotte said, trying to put a quick end to Sheriff Wainwright's interrogation of her. It certainly felt like an interrogation, and she was already running interference for Brenda, who, she told the sheriff, was in no condition at the moment to answer questions on David Runion's death. "You know Brenda couldn't have done this. She's been laid up in bed with ankle sprains since yesterday afternoon."

"Actually, I don't personally know that. You've been keeping me away from her."

"I can attest that she is immobile," Evonne Clagett broke in. "I treated her, And I can tell you that she won't be up for a couple of more days."

They were sitting at one of the tables in the retirement center's dining room. Others, including deputy sheriffs, home staff members, and residents—even an FBI agent or two because of the sighting of Ida Smith—were milling around the room. Although the body of the elderly actor had been taken down from the chandelier and removed, his wheelchair remained turned over under the light fixture and yellow police tape circled the center of the foyer. Brenda was still in bed back at the house, where Tony and Michelle were tending to her. She knew that Runion was dead, but they were trying to delay telling her the details. It was just too similar to the way Helga Lund, Brenda's former significant other, had died, a murder for which Brenda had been suspected for several months.

"One of the residents, Gladys Morrison, has given the testimony—" Sheriff Wainwright began to say, returning to his very stilted, formal view of investigation.

"Gladys is a fruitcake, and a malevolent one at that," Charlotte snapped. "And I should know. She was my mother-in-law for longer than I could take it."

"Nevertheless, when she first saw the body of David Runion, according to several witnesses, she implicated Brenda Boynton and she also mentioned something about financial gain. Are you denying she did that?"

"No, I'm not denying that," Charlotte said. "But that's all water under the bridge. Gladys worked for the Hollywood costume designer, Helga Lund, and has always blamed Brenda for that woman's death, even long after Brenda was cleared of that and the murderer was brought to justice. On the money front, yes, the retirement center benefits financially in David's death—the retirement center, not Brenda. David has left most of his fortune to the community. But you'd have to be crazy—which Gladys Morrison is—to think that Brenda would have had anything to do with David's death. She doesn't need anyone's money; she has more than enough of her own. And the mere suggestion that she could lift him up on the chandelier to begin with, even if her ankles weren't sprained, which they are, is utterly ridiculous. Have you ruled out suicide? David was not going into the dark night of dementia easily. Yesterday was a lucid day for him. Maybe he just assessed his position and decide to check out."

"You don't really believe he committed suicide do you?" Margaret Fancel, the FBI agent sitting at the table, who also had been Charlotte's assistant when Charlotte worked in the Annapolis office, asked quietly. Evan Worthington had wanted to come, but Charlotte had told him in no uncertain terms not to—that the presence of someone that senior from the FBI would make Sheriff Wainwright belligerent. Well, more belligerent than usual. Worthington had done the next best thing; he'd sent the agent Charlotte was most comfortable working with and who could help Charlotte keep her balance.

"No, I can't see a man in a wheelchair capable of doing that," Charlotte said, calming down. She was grateful to Margaret for bringing her back to center.

"No," the sheriff said. "It looked like there was a feeble effort to raise the possibility of suicide, but it's more like someone wanted us to know that they'd murdered the man. You'd need the use of strong legs to do that, to hang a man on a chandelier like that. Not something a man in a wheelchair could do unless he was faking it."

"No, I agree not," Charlotte said. She knew that David Runion had not been faking his need for a wheelchair. She had watched him slowly deteriorate over the past year and a half. She decided to change tack.

"But let's just forget that a woman with two sprained ankles could do it either. What I want to know, though, is what's being done about finding Ida Smith? She's the known dangerous criminal in this equation. And she's a wiry one. I'll bet she was strong enough to do that to David Runion. If she's been hiding under our noses as a staff physical therapist here, as Evonne says she has been doing, she probably overheard what happened to Helga Lund and is just toying with us with the method of killing David."

"But why would she kill Runion?" the sheriff asked.

"To cover her tracks. Have your men found her?"

"No."

"Well, there you go. She's taken good advantage of the diversion then. hasn't she?"

"But why would she still be around at all?" the sheriff asked. "If she was here looking for the bank heist money, knowing it was here somewhere but not knowing exactly where, why didn't she leave when we found it?"

"Does anyone at the retirement home know you found the money?" Charlotte asked. "Did you release that information yet? I certainly haven't told anyone."

"No, I guess not," Wainwright said.

"Well, if that's all the silly questioning you have for me or Brenda at the moment," Charlotte said, as she stood up from the table, "don't let me keep you from the effort to find Ida Smith. As for me, I'm going to go find Gladys Morrison and strangle her."

Wainwright knitted his brow and frowned, and both Margaret Fancel and Evonne Clagett looked a little distressed at that pronouncement. Sam and Rocket, who had been laying at Charlotte's feet, perked up, though. They too stood, ready to go wherever Charlotte was going—and help their mistress do whatever she wanted to do.

Charlotte wasn't pulling privilege by having the dogs with her inside the retirement center. That was one of a few instances in which

Brenda had veered off course from most nursing homes when setting this one up. In interviewing possible residents, time and again she had run up against people who should be going into institutional independent or assisted living facilities but who were unwilling to do so because they would not abandon their closest companions in their declining years, their pets. Brenda quickly had negated that by allowing pets, within reason, and by hiring a couple of veterinarian medicine students part time from the University of Maryland to help take care of them.

Charlotte didn't find Gladys, though, and didn't really put much effort into doing so. She was chagrined with herself for having lost her composure like that concerning Gladys around the sheriff and her friends. She knew it didn't increase her credibility about Gladys' accusation by calling the woman what she was—a nasty old nut. Sheriff Wainwright had the sort of effect on her, however, that brought out her fighting edge. She had found him engaging in some minor corruption more than a year earlier. Neither of them had taken that any farther, but they had remained tense with each other ever since.

Rather than going after Gladys after she had cooled down, Charlotte went to the locker that had been assigned to Ida Smith, which Evonne had opened for the authorities, found a sweater there, and ran it under Sam and Rocket's noses. She told them this belonged to a bad woman and they needed to find her, feeling silly about doing so, but not having any other ideas. The dogs gave her intelligent looks like they understood what she wanted—which only made her laugh and feel more silly.

Nevertheless, Charlotte took them out into the compound at the end of the point and walked them all around, more wishing than hoping that they'd run Ida to ground. She was surprised and laughed again when they showed a great deal of interest in a shovel in a garden shed. Rather than assuring her that the dogs were on the trail of the missing woman, that made her feel that she was wasting her time, until she remembered the digging at the Thompson house and decided, as a face-saving thought, that the dogs smelled Ida on the shovel. Other than this she'd come up empty, though, and she decided she needed to go back to Brenda now. She hadn't seen Brenda since before Brenda was given the news of David Runion's death.

Charlotte rounded the corner of the retirement facility, headed for the forecourt and the entrance gate. Just in time she saw a gabbling cluster of the media arriving. Someone had blabbed about the death of David Runion, and the deluge of the press had begun. Front and center in the group was Ron Rendel, a top investigative reporter with the *Baltimore Sun* with whom Charlotte had played a cat-and-mouse game of "guess what I know" on and off, contrasted occasionally with close cooperation, ever since Charlotte's days with the Annapolis FBI office. Charlotte waited until the reporters had entered the building before she headed back toward the road out of the compound, but she saw out of the corner of her eye that Rendel had held back. He seemed to be putting out the butt of a cigarette, though, and she didn't think he saw her, so she made a quiet dash for the road, shushing the dogs, who cooperated by not making a sound.

As she came out of what was the current front gate into the retirement community compound, which would be moved when the compound was enlarged to take in the buildings up to Charlotte's cottage, Sam and Rocket barked and pulled on the leash. She assumed they realized they were going home, because that was the direction they were pulling her in. But when Charlotte raised her head and looked up River Street, she saw a figure emerge from the cellar of her cottage through doors set over an outside staircase leading down into the space.

The figure saw her and the dogs too—and began to run.

It was Ida Smith. Charlotte, who had been hunting the woman for years wasn't fooled any longer by the darker hair color or the glasses.

The direction that Ida ran in was across River Street into the Thompson property, where she had lived as a girl, and then around the side of what was now a hole in the ground and toward the tree-lined back of the lot. Sam and Rocket, barking up a storm, were pulling Charlotte along at an angle that would intersect with Ida before the woman could make it to the tree line. But Ida was thin and wiry and Charlotte most certainly was not. As they both raced along in what seemed to be an eternity but was less than thirty seconds, Charlotte realized that Ida was gaining ground and that she, Charlotte, was just dead weight for the straining dogs.

Charlotte dropped Sam's and Rocket's leashes and let them run on their own.

Ida was already at the tree line and disappearing into the thick brush and closely placed trees. Sam and Rocket were there not long afterward.

There was no cry or splash that Charlotte heard, but when she'd managed to push her way through the clinging tree branches and sticking bush nettles, she probably would have plunged into the murky waters of the salt pond behind the houses herself if Sam and Rocket hadn't been sitting on the bank and looking down into the water.

Ida had hit her head on a protruding sharp large tree branch sticking out of the pond and very well may have been dead before she even slipped into the water. It was clear that she hadn't tried to get out of the water. Although Charlotte found that the pond bottom was deep in clutching mud and dead leaves when she waded in to pull Ida's body out, the pond wasn't deep. If Ida had been alive—or conscious—when she went in, she could have stood up in the pond and her head would have been above the water.

But Charlotte didn't know any of this before she went into the water herself. She had to assume that Ida was still alive. She wasn't sure the woman wasn't until she got her back up on the pond bank.

The dogs sat patiently and showed a great deal of interest in Charlotte's technique as she slipped and slid around on the slick pond bottom and had to take three runs at pulling the body up onto the bank. When she had done so and turned Ida over on her back, Charlotte could see that any efforts to revive her would be fruitless.

Exhausted after she had achieved this, Charlotte laid down with the body between her and the dogs, panting more heavily than either one of them was doing. She muttered, "What are you two looking at?"

But she couldn't be upset with them. Somehow the sweater scent bit had gotten through to them. If they hadn't barked as Charlotte was bringing them out of the compound entrance, Ida probably would have had time to draw back out of sight before Charlotte saw her.

Charlotte reclined there for several minutes. She knew she had to trudge back to the retirement center and raise the police, but to do so at this moment—and the condition her clothes were in—would be a major photo and story op for the press. And she shuddered to think what they'd do with everything happening at Curtain Call today. It might be enough to close it—and put an end to Brenda's dreams. A real tragedy for Brenda on top of losing her old friend David Runion in the process.

Charlotte had to think of some end run around the press.

And then it was no longer an option.

"My this is interesting," a male voice said from just inside the trees at the side of the pond. And then the reporter, Ron Rendel, emerged onto the narrow bank.

"It's not what you think," Charlotte said dully.

"I was thinking you were having a friendly picnic, so I'm quite prepared to believe it's not what I think. I must admit I was quite amused watching you lope across the lawns after this woman, but it doesn't seem quite so funny now. May I assume you didn't do her in?"

"No, she did herself in."

"Is that a good thing?"

"In many ways it's a very good thing, Ron. And I'll tell you all about it—an exclusive before the others get it—if you will go back to the center, find Deputy Dave Burch, and very quietly tell him I'm out here with the body of Ida Smith and if you can do it without alerting any of your media colleagues."

"Ida Smith. That almost rings a bell."

"It should. And it's worth an exclusive. As you can see, It wouldn't be the best idea for me to walk into the middle of a press conference. Deputy Dave Burch, avoiding Sheriff Haws Wainwright, if you can."

After Rendel departed and before Dave Burch, Evonne Clagett, Margaret Fancel, and a couple of deputies showed up, Charlotte had the time to realize that she felt a bit depressed rather than the elation she had expected she'd feel when Ida Smith was finally caught.

It was an ending, she realized. And more of a final curtain than a curtain call. For the first time she felt completely retired and no longer in the FBI game. Ida Smith was her last open case. She was done now.

* * * *

Dave Burch let Charlotte take the dogs home as well as urging her to take a shower and change before coming back. There was no doubt she'd have to talk to Sheriff Wainwright, but he was giving a press conference at the moment and neither of them thought he'd be impressed if Charlotte walked into that looking like some creature that had risen from the swamp.

Charlotte spent only a few minutes with Brenda, but it was long enough that Brenda made her reveal how David Runion had died.

"I knew it was something like that—because Tony wouldn't tell me more than that he was dead. He wasn't the least convincing when he said it had been an accident. An actor may be able to fool an audience, but not another actor. I'm sorry that someone took his life, but I'm glad it wasn't suicide. I couldn't bear to think he was unhappy about being here." Her voice was weak, and this seemed to have taken all of her energy out of her.

"Nothing like that, Brenda. You treated him like a king and he knew you did. When I wheeled him back to his cottage yesterday, he told me how much you meant to him." What he'd said was in another context altogether, but Charlotte thought, what the hell, that's what Brenda deserved to hear from the man. He hadn't appreciated her nearly enough in life; he jolly well could make up for that in death.

Brenda didn't turn down the offer of sleeping pills and was asleep again before Charlotte turned the dogs over to Bea in the kitchen and headed back out to the retirement center.

She entered the center by the kitchen, intending to go on through to the dining room, where the press conference was being conducted, as quietly and unobtrusively as possible. The grumpy four were plastered up against the door from the kitchen to the dining room, though, eavesdropping on the press conference.

Seeing Charlotte enter from the outside, Gladys Morrison broke off from the others and was in Charlotte's face before she could retreat.

"I know a secret, I do. And it's one you would really like to hear."

"Gladys, I don't have time for your games now. We can talk later."

"Just you think about it until we do," Gladys said. "Just you think about things not being as they seem and that making all of the difference. It's all in train now. I don't think you have the brains to stop it." She cackled then and returned to her vigil with the other three.

Charlotte was suddenly just too tired to face the press or Haws Wainwright or anyone else. She turned and slipped back out of the kitchen by the door to the delivery dock. She went straight home in the gathering gloom, grabbed a fast sandwich prepared by Bea that, of course, was gourmet despite the zero notice, and went upstairs, undressed, and crawled into bed beside Brenda. She took Brenda in her arms. Brenda was too far gone to notice, but Charlotte needed something real and important to her to hang onto in those moments. And nothing did that better than Brenda did just by being there.

* * * *

This time the call in the middle of the night came in the form of heavy rapping on the front door. The dogs pushed their way out of the bedroom door and onto the hall landing and harmonized their howls. Tony, in a dressing gown, was half way down the stairs and Michelle was standing in their bedroom doorway when Charlotte, tying off her own robe, came out of her bedroom. Brenda was so drugged she didn't stir.

As Tony opened the front door, Sheriff Haws Wainwright pushed his way in.

"Is Charlotte Diamond here?" he asked in a gruff voice.

"Yes, I'm here," Charlotte said as she came down the stairs.

"And have you been here all evening and night?"

"Yes, of course. I'm sorry I didn't stay around to give you my testimony on the death of Ida Smith. But I was exhausted. It's completely my responsibility. I didn't give Dave Burch an opportunity to say otherwise. But can't we do this tomorrow—or later today, I guess. In the daylight?"

"Forget the Smith woman for now. Is there anyone else who can verify you've been here all evening and night?"

"I doubt it," Charlotte said. "I was in bed, sleeping." Charlotte didn't tell him that Brenda had been in the same bed. She didn't see that as any of his business, assuming he didn't already know the score on that. And it wouldn't have helped anyway. Brenda had been even more totally zonked out than she was.

"I can verify it," Tony said. "She's had a rough day, and I've checked in on her periodically. She's been in bed since shortly after she ate her dinner."

"And she had her bit of dinner just before six—and then went right to her room. I've checked in on her—and on Ms. Brenda a couple of times—into the night, in case either one woke up early and wanted a proper dinner." Bea had quite delicately neither lied nor revealed that the women had been sleeping in the same room.

"I can verify Charlotte was here too," Michelle said as she descended the staircase.

"Are you going to claim you went to her room to check her presence out as well?" Wainwright asked with a sarcastic tone. "That's one heap of checking. Did you three do it in relay so you could account for every fifteen minutes?" His voice was dripping with sarcasm and disbelief.

"No, not really. Charlotte snored," Michelle responded in a much sweeter tone.

It was all Charlotte could do to keep from laughing. As it was Tony did snort. "Sorry, Charlotte," he said. "But Michelle's right. You *were* snoring. I didn't have to actually look in the bedroom to know you were there."

"Can you please tell us what this is all about, Haws?" Charlotte said, turning to the sheriff. "Why the third degree?"

"Gladys Morrison is dead. She was strangled in her cottage sometime in the late evening or early morning hours. And you very publicly threatened to kill her—by strangling her."

"Well, shit," Charlotte exclaimed after they'd all taken a long moment to process that information. "Sorry, I'm sure there must be some folks who would be upset by that news, but how likely is it that a former FBI agent like me would declare in a room full of policeman that I was going to murder someone and then go right ahead and do it?"

"I suppose," Wainwright said, while still giving her a hard, suspicious stare. "But I want to take your statement—and the supporting ones of your crew here too."

"Well, you'd best come in then," Charlotte said.

Ever the efficient hostess, Bea chimed in, "Why don't you all come back to the den. It's more comfortable. I'll put on some coffee."

After the statements, as the sheriff was departing, Charlotte stopped him in the foyer, when it was just the two of them present, Wainwright and Charlotte. "You know how this complicates everything, don't you?" Charlotte asked.

"How's that?" Wainwright answered.

"It means that the murders—certainly Gladys' but probably David Runion's as well—can't be pinned all nice and neat on Ida Smith. Ida was already dead when Gladys was killed. I saw and talked with Gladys after Ida died." Charlotte wasn't quite ready to tell what Gladys said to her on that occasion, though. Charlotte wanted more time to mull that over herself, which is pretty much what occupied her mind all the next day, when she wasn't answering calls and giving Ron Rendel that exclusive interview she'd promised him for the *Baltimore Sun*.

It was Wainwright's turn to say "Well, shit" now. "It must be someone else at the retirement center then," he said as he walked out the door.

"Yes, it must," Charlotte agreed. But somehow it all had to make sense too—and now the death of Gladys had to fit in with the rest. It was a puzzle, and Charlotte couldn't resist puzzles.

And there was something in what Haws had said earlier that, when combined with the last thing Gladys said to her, Charlotte thought just might be a key piece to this puzzle.

* * * *

Charlotte was restless the next night. There was something she needed to check out after all of the cogitating she'd done that day, and if her hunch was right, it would open this whole mystery up. Brenda was in a deep sleep again, produced by sleeping pills. She'd declared this was the last night she'd take them. She was terrified of becoming addicted to anything as she'd seen too many of her colleagues in movies become. Her ankles weren't giving her as much pain anymore. It was more now the pain in her heart that was keeping her awake.

After tossing and turning for a couple of hours, Charlotte decided that a sleeping pill might be the answer for her as well and she rolled out of bed and went through the dressing room to the bathroom beyond. She'd left the pills on the counter, and the light of a full moon was streaming in through the bathroom window, so she didn't turn the light on.

A slight noise caused her to turn and look through the dressing room into the bedroom. A figure was stealing across the foot of the bed toward Brenda's side.

Making as little noise as possible, Charlotte moved into the dressing room and picked up the first heavy object her hand encountered. Then it was on into the bedroom.

The figure was creeping around the end of the bed, arms extended, the moonlight streaming into the bedroom through a window reflecting off the length of wire held taunt between the fists. Two quiet steps, a swing of the object in her hand way back, and a flash forward with it, and the Wellington boot heel connected with Phil Taylor's head. He dropped to the floor like a rock.

No respectable former FBI agent fails to have a hand gun and a couple of handcuffs in her nightstand drawer, so by the time her shouts roused Tony and Michelle and even Brenda was coming to, Charlotte had cuffs on the former movie cameraman's wrists and ankles, dumped him in a chair, and asked Tony to cover him with her handgun while she called the sheriff's office.

Later, after the sheriff's deputies had hauled Taylor—the supposedly wheelchair-bound quarter of the four grumps—away, all of those in the household, including a somewhat groggy Brenda, were sitting in front of the fireplace in the den drinking the coffee and eating the muffins that Bea had provided. She'd even prepared doggie treats for Sam and Rocket, who were somewhat confused that people were up and not taking them for a walk but who settled down quickly enough on recognizing that humans just were not predictable in their behavior and were so hard to train.

"You didn't seem surprised it was the cameraman," Tony said to Charlotte.

"Not by last night," Charlotte said. "I reasoned, after Ida Smith was eliminated, that it must be one of the four grumps. They all had grudges against Brenda. And it all started with Brenda's two accidents, which weren't accidents. We just didn't see that at the time. Brenda even told us she thought she was pulled down the steps the second time, and we just didn't pay attention to that. None of those four were grateful to Brenda for letting them come here. They all openly hated her—and they fed each other's hate. Phil Taylor's hatred was probably deeper than the others. He thought that Brenda had taken Helga Lund from him and then allowed her to be killed, even if she didn't do it herself, which for months he did believe. And he blamed her for having gotten fired from the studio as well and having to start up his own business."

"But the wheelchair—" Tony began.

"Yes, that hit me in the face more than once. The wheelchair was the only thing preventing Phil Taylor from popping out as the most likely suspect. And it was enough to eliminate him from the beginning. Very clever that. But even the sheriff, who isn't the sharpest knife in the drawer, said something about a wheelchair being an excuse for immobility if the need for it wasn't being faked. He said that about David, but as soon as I recalled him saying that, I realized it fit Taylor as well. None of us had any knowledge confirming he needed a wheelchair. He was hurt right before he was fired when he went off the cliff—but, Brenda, chances are good that he tried to do you in even then. He might have been trying to push you off the cliff—but there's no evidence that he didn't fully recover from that fall."

"You said you knew it was one of the grumpy four," Michelle said.

"Yes, after Ida Smith wasn't a candidate, I had to think of another reason why it had happened. That's when it dawned on me that there were attempts to hurt Brenda under our very eyes. And the death of David Runion, especially in the way it was done, could be seen as a particularly cruel attack on Brenda. David himself had told me to watch out for the four. The natural suspicion then was on Stan Plaugher. The two women probably weren't strong enough to lift David up the ladder—they found the step ladder under the stairs; it shouldn't have been there. And Paul Taylor was in a wheelchair.

"The kicker was in rationalizing the death of Gladys. She'd taunted me about knowing something—involving something that wasn't what it seemed. And then she died before she could tell me what it was. Anyone who knew Gladys knew she couldn't keep a secret and that she would tell me eventually. And only the four grumps were in the kitchen when she told me that. So, it logically was one of the other three who was the murderer. Once I questioned the need for a wheelchair, that became the logical thing that wasn't what it seemed. Killing Gladys wouldn't be part of the series of attacks on Brenda; it therefore must have been an act of self-preservation by the murderer."

"Well, the guy certainly seemed shocked that you were in the bedroom tonight, as well," Michelle said. She was smiling. Charlotte could have hugged her for her casual tolerance.

"Yep, he certainly didn't do his research," she answered, with a laugh.

"And that, sports fans, is why I never intend to sleep alone again," Brenda piped up and said. And then she added, giving a meaningful look at Charlotte, "It's also why I never intend on giving my Wellington boots up."

All laughed, but only Charlotte and Brenda knew the full context of that remark.

Later, after everyone had gone back to bed except Brenda and Charlotte and the two dogs and the two women were cuddling on the sofa, Brenda said in a soft, contemplative voice, "Losing David like that certainly puts an ending on one phase of my life. I pursued him for decades—through multiple curtain calls, both in the movies and in life. And now that phase is over. I thought I was establishing Curtain Call

150

primarily for him. To have him nearby even though I have, without reservation, chosen you."

The two took a few minutes to do more than cuddle.

"So, your interest in the retirement community has waned?" Charlotte asked.

"Oh, no, it hasn't in the least. His passing has made me realize that my interest was much larger than that. I was concentrating on endings—that's why, I'm sure, I thought of calling the community Curtain Call. And I was trying to take the high road on that or I would have called it Final Curtain, and no movie person in his or her right mind would have ever come here. We are—despite those grumpy four—optimistic folk in the theater. We are looking to the next movie premier and the new scripts and the opportunities to be greater, to shine brighter."

"My, where is all of this leading?" Charlotte asked.

"I think it's leading beyond a curtain call in our lives, Charlotte. I think of where we are as a beginning, a curtain rise, not any form of ending. What I'm saying, Charlotte, is I think we should get married— we can do that legally in Maryland now. I think we should make the full commitment. Am I saying anything that you can't commit to, that you don't want? Because if I am, it's OK, we can continue to—"

That's as far as Brenda got, because, quickly recovering from the shock of the proposal, Charlotte was now showing Brenda just how totally OK that proposal was with her.

About the Author

Olivia Stowe is a published author under different names and in other dimensions of fiction and nonfiction and lives quietly in a university town with an indulgent spouse.

Mystery Romance
Restoring the Castle

The Charlotte Diamond mystery series
By The Howling
Retired with Prejudice
Coast to Coast
An Inconvenient Death
What's The Point?
White Orchid Found
Curtain Call
Making Room at Christmas (Seasonal Special)

The Savannah Series
Chatham Square
Savannah Time

Olivia's Inspirational Christmas collections
Christmas Seconds (2011)
Spirit of Christmas (2010)